Far From Heaven

Look for these titles by
Cherrie Lynn

Now Available:

Unleashed

Rock Me

Sweet Disgrace

Far From Heaven

Far From Heaven

Cherrie Lynn

SAMHAIN
PUBLISHING

Samhain Publishing, Ltd.
11821 Mason Montgomery Road, 4B
Cincinnati, OH 45249
www.samhainpublishing.com

Far From Heaven
Copyright © 2012 by Cherrie Lynn
Print ISBN: 978-1-60928-436-7
Digital ISBN: 978-1-60928-432-9

Editing by Linda Ingmanson
Cover by Kanaxa

First Samhain Publishing, Ltd. electronic publication: April 2011
First Samhain Publishing, Ltd. print publication: March 2012

Dedication

For my mom, who completely rocks and is in *no* way an inspiration for some of my heroines' wretched mothers (and yes, she's asked me this before). She believes in me, encourages me, and most importantly, she's very proud of me. If not for her, I wouldn't be doing this. I love you, Mom!

Prologue

Twenty-seven years ago

The knock on the door sounded innocent enough. Pleasant, even. Light and friendly.

It wasn't.

The man sitting at the battered old desk seemed to know that. His balding head jerked up from the lines he was snorting with a rolled-up dollar bill, and he blanched whiter than the powder scattered across the scarred desktop. Whiter than the wife-beater he wore...which, come to that, wasn't all that white, but torn and yellowed with sweat stains.

Apparently he at least suspected that death was standing outside his door. What he didn't realize was that a far more dangerous foe sat watching the scene from the tattered living room couch, cloaked in invisibility.

Ashemnon narrowed his eyes as the man leapt from his chair and stared at the front door with the whites of his eyes showing all around blue irises—though his pupils were so dilated the blue was nearly eclipsed by discs of black.

Blue, like her eyes will be.

Ash fidgeted as impatience gnawed at him. He wanted to get this show on the road, but not quite yet. Better to let the man's fear build to a fever pitch, to a point of desperation that would impel him to do anything, pay any price, for his life to be spared. He was in bad trouble with worse people...people who would knock on your door and shoot you in the face. Without any sort of intervention, he was going to die here, now, riddled with bullets and left to rot until someone complained about the smell and sent management to investigate. This was the sort of seedy establishment that housed hollow-eyed tenants who normally didn't see you as long as you pretended not to see them.

It didn't matter one way or another to Ash what happened to the waste of life currently rummaging through a desk drawer as silently as he could. But the man—whose name was Gatlin—possessed something he wanted, something he *needed*, and a moment like this was when he would be most likely to part with it for the promise of deliverance.

The knock sounded again, more insistent this time. The human jerked a pistol out of the drawer and plastered his back to the cracked drywall. Inch by inch, he crept along toward the door, staying out of the line of sight of anyone who might begin shooting from the opposite side.

As dust floated lazily in the single dingy shaft of sunlight slanting through a grime-encrusted window, Gatlin's breathing threatened to go out of control and Ash imagined he could hear the mortal's heart pounding. Given the several hundred milligrams of cocaine bubbling through the man's bloodstream, it was amazing a heart attack wouldn't fell him before the bullets could.

The idiot was opening his mouth to call out to the person at the door.

Now. Ash dropped the shields that kept him invisible to human eyes and threw up one that would protect them both from being heard, wrapping himself and his target in a protective cocoon separate from the time and space of the human's realm.

The clock on the wall stopped ticking. The rush of traffic outside the thin walls ceased. Absolute silence descended.

Blinking, Gatlin looked around, his brow furrowing...until his gaze fell on Ash lounging on his couch. Then his eyes flew even wider, and he swung the weapon up and pointed it directly at Ash's chest.

Ash only grinned. "You're going to die."

"Fuck you," Gatlin rasped and opened fire.

One...two...three...four...

Ash made a show of yawning as the man succeeded only in putting six neat bullet holes in the back of the couch. It hadn't been a quality item in the first place, brown and stained and leaking more stuffing than it contained. Ash sighed and crossed his ankle over his knee as Gatlin continued frantically pulling the trigger until it merely clicked.

"Are you quite done?"

"How the...who the hell...?" Gatlin's nostrils flared with every loud, desperate breath. The gun fell from his seemingly nerveless fingers and clunked on the floor.

"I'm not who *you* think I am, obviously. Or else I would be bleeding out on your floor, would I not?" Ash allowed his upper lip to curl. This was the fun part. "I'd hate to know that hideous vomit-colored carpet was about to become the last thing I beheld. But here's the thing, Gatlin...you're about to get up close and personal with it. You're two minutes away from watching it go red with your blood as the life pumps out of your body. The man standing on the other side of that door will blow so many new holes through you, my friend, I'll be able to look through you and see daylight on the other side." For dramatic effect, he stood and began pacing slowly toward the blubbering

11

man, never blinking, never letting him escape his gaze. Gatlin slid down the wall, muttering nonsense, his fists clenching and unclenching spasmodically as his chin fell to his chest.

Ash fought down a surge of renewed revulsion. He was almost tempted to end negotiations before they began. End them, and let this scourge on humanity eat lead. His was a soul Ash could reap on the spot, no questions asked. No angels would be coming to wing him to his rest.

But it wasn't *his* soul he wanted right now. Gatlin...he was too easy. Drugs, assault, burglary, rape. Hell would be welcoming him with open arms eventually, and right now Ash's superiors were content to let Gatlin carry on doing his dirty work upon the earth. Ash didn't plan on making any provisions regarding the man's afterlife. This was all about saving his ass *now*.

The soul Ash was really here to collect was one he ordinarily couldn't touch.

Gatlin looked as if he was about to pass out. With the toe of one black boot, Ash tilted his chin up. The man's eyes rolled upward, his bleary gaze finally focusing.

"Get up."

The stuttering began to form words. "Hail Mary, full of grace, the Lord is—"

Ash gave him a mouthful of boot leather, knocking his head hard against the wall. "I'm sure she has more deserving sinners to pray for. I said get *up*." Without waiting for him to try, Ash leaned over and hauled him up by the front of his shirt, half-tearing it in the process—the man was damn near dead weight. Ash deposited him in a nearby chair that was in worse shape than the couch, then sat across from him on the scarred coffee table. Gatlin watched in slack-jawed fear as Ash rested his elbows on his knees, steepled his fingers at his lips and simply stared.

"Wh-what do you want from me?" Gatlin stammered. A trickle of blood ran from his busted lower lip.

"It's quite simple, really. I want to save you."

Gatlin swiped at the blood on his face, then stared at the stark crimson on his fingers. The blow had apparently knocked some sense into him. Or at the very least, sobered him up a bit. "You've got a hell of a way of showing it, pal."

Ash grinned at that. "Indeed. I won't sugarcoat things. You're in a dire situation, Maxwell Gatlin, and for a price, I'll get you out of it. This time."

"What?"

"I don't like repeating myself, and I won't tolerate stupid questions. Use what little brain you haven't fried. I appeared out of thin air. Every bullet you fired should have pierced my chest, but you murdered your couch instead." He grinned again, letting heat gather behind his eyes so they would burn red. Gatlin clumsily tried to scramble back in his chair. "Yet here I sit, offering you a chance to escape certain death. And make no mistake, death is certain today unless you accept my help."

"All right, man, I get it. If you can get me out, fucking do it already."

"Ah, but I haven't even named my price."

"Name it." Gatlin glanced back at the door as if he expected it to burst open at any moment in a rain of gunfire.

All amusement left Ash's demeanor. He felt it drain at the thought of *her*, felt the muscles of his throat constrict. The words tore loose in a strangled growl. "Your daughter."

Gatlin's incredulous gaze swung back around to him. "You got the wrong guy. I ain't got no daughter."

13

"That you know of." He watched the man's face slacken. "Her name is Madeleine. She's six months old." Ash leaned over until they were almost nose to nose, only a few inches separating them. "And I want her."

He could see the calculations going on behind Gatlin's eyes, trying to figure out who he'd knocked up well over a year ago. Now wasn't the time for him to have an attack of conscience.

"What does it matter to you?" Ash asked. "Her mother was a prostitute whose fee you stiffed and then forced anyway. Not an uncommon occurrence for you, if I understand correctly. So, congratulations. But why would you possibly give a damn? It's not as if the kid would have anything to do with you, even if her mother let her. Just another person in your life to someday tell you what a slimy piece of shit you are. Do you really need one more?"

Gatlin just stared dumbly. Ash leaned back and feigned nonchalance. "Of course, you can always protect her and fulfill your fate, which is to drown in your own blood after getting punched full of bullet holes. I can't promise a quick end. I think you'll feel every hit, and then you'll have the agony of—"

"Stop! I'll do it. You can have the girl. I won't ever know her anyways."

At the proclamation, Ash felt the weight of centuries of longing lift off him and he felt almost...free. Happy, even. He wanted to hang his head in exhausted relief, but he kept it high, kept his gaze steady on the man before him who'd just handed him everything he'd been chasing for a long, long time.

Standing, he reached into the inside pocket of his black coat and pulled out the contract he'd drafted stating the terms of the bargain. He unfurled it on the coffee table, holding it flat so Gatlin could read. It was quite a simple one. The girl's soul, taken at a time of Ash's choosing, but not before her twenty-fifth birthday—Hell had no interest in younger souls; they weren't tainted enough. In exchange, Ash would immediately remove him from one and only one situation that would end in his death. He watched Gatlin's gaze move intently across the parchment as he read. When he was done, he looked up, his jaw tense.

"How do I sign?"

Ash produced a quill from his pocket and gestured for Gatlin to give him his hand. He gasped when Ash drew a fingernail across the back, slicing it open and releasing a thin ribbon of blood. Without further explanation, he held out the quill.

Blowing out a breath, Gatlin took it, drew it through his own blood. And signed over his unknown daughter's soul to a demon.

Ash grinned as he snatched the parchment away and pressed his thumb to the bottom, leaving an intricately scripted *A* sizzling and smoking once he lifted it away. The hands on the clock whirred forward, the sunlight in the room quickly melted to darkness except for a faint red neon glow from well outside the window. Any armed assailants were long gone.

"Now," he said, quickly rolling up the precious document, "I suggest you get out of here before someone comes back."

Gatlin nodded vigorously, looking as if he wanted to go down on his knees in front of him. His words were as breathless as if he'd just run ten miles. "Thank you. Fuck. Thank you so much."

Ash turned his back and strolled toward the door, tucking the scroll safely in his coat. She was his. At last. "Save your thanks, Gatlin. I'm sure we'll be seeing you soon enough."

15

Chapter One

"Damn, damn, *damn*." Maddie staggered on her heels as she scurried down the sidewalk. She was late again. Again. How the hell it had happened, she had no idea, but David was not going to be thrilled. She could almost hear his reprimand echoing in her head.

She rounded a corner and the restaurant swung into view, separated from her by a steady whizzing stream of city traffic. With her gaze anxiously locked on the red Do Not Walk light, she reached the post and furiously thumbed the button.

"Come on, come on." Her newly reset watch read seven twenty-one. Over twenty minutes late. Oh, forget not thrilled— David was going to be *livid*. She'd tried to call his cell, but he hadn't answered. Whether he'd silenced it out of respect for the other restaurant patrons or he was just ignoring her, she didn't know.

David seemed to care an awful lot about what other people thought of him...except, it seemed, for her. Their entire relationship was balanced on a knife's edge, teetering toward the side of peril all the time. She feared one nudge might send it crashing, but she was probably only being paranoid. God knew it wouldn't be the first time.

Tonight, she'd been hoping they could talk about what they

could do to change things. She was going to tell him how wretched he'd been making her feel lately and, if all went well, they'd sort through it and end up back at his place. Laughing and watching old movies and making love all night, the way they used to in the beginning, when things were good.

Well, that was the fantasy. Now it was shot all to hell.

The light changed and she all but sprinted across the street—as well as she could in these freaking heels, anyway. She was accustomed to sneakers and flip-flops, and already her arches were screaming, "Woman, are you *insane?*"

Her mad dash up the steps took what remaining breath she had, and she could hardly tell the host that she was meeting someone who'd already arrived. What if David had grown tired of waiting around and left? Oh God, that would be so humiliating. But she couldn't say she'd blame him.

A sigh of relief escaped her after she told the man David's name and he turned to lead her toward the back of the restaurant, in the direction of their favorite table. Whew, he was still here. Fuming, no doubt, but depending on his mood, he might get over it in a few minutes and they could enjoy their evening. He was a firm believer in punctuality and often chastised her about being one of the most unorganized people he'd ever met.

Well, she thought sadly, there was really no use denying it. It almost seemed as if something was *preventing* her from being anything other than a woman with a complete inability to get her shit together. As if some kind of cosmic prankster was constantly shadowing her, throwing monkey wrenches into her life. And it was all coming to a head, about to culminate in...something. She didn't know what, but it was nothing good. All her life, she'd lived with the sense that the axe was poised and ready to fall. It was only a question of when and where and

17

how many necks it was going to sever.

David's sandy-blond head came into view and she fortified her resolve with a deep breath as she stepped around the table and dropped into the chair the host pulled out for her, the apology already forming on her lips. When she lifted her gaze from David's slowly drumming fingers to the anger simmering in his eyes, the words died before she could lend them voice.

In her lap, she twisted her fingers together. She bit her lip for a second and tried again. "David, I'm—"

"What was it this time? Flat tire? Wardrobe malfunction? Alien abduction?"

All my clocks were wrong. All of them.

She knew how crazy it would make her sound if she spoke the truth, that she'd thought she was right on time until she left her apartment, got into her Jeep and saw the time on the radio display. *Weird,* she'd thought. It must've been running fast. Then she'd seen it on the sign as she drove past the bank up the street from her house. And heard the DJ say it on the radio.

Giving up on an explanation that would satisfy him, she shrugged. "All I can say is I'm sorry."

"It wouldn't be such a big deal if it didn't happen *all the time.*"

"I get that you're upset, and I even deserve it, but don't you think we could talk about this some other—"

He seemed to pretend she wasn't even speaking. "I don't get you. The biggest problem is you're getting worse."

"I'm getting...worse?"

"You're never on time, you're absentminded, clumsy, the nightmares are getting more intense and you're seeing things. I think it's time you went to talk to someone, Maddie. I mean it."

Her eyes flew wide and her fingers clamped together hard

enough to nearly snap the bones. She found it impossible to swallow around the horror lodged in her throat. "You're saying you think I need a *shrink*? You think I'm crazy?"

"I didn't say you were crazy. Don't put words in my mouth."

"What else am I supposed to glean from that?" The truth was, given everything he'd just described, she would think the very same thing if their positions were reversed. That he needed help.

But she didn't like thinking about the nightmares. Or about some of the other things that had been happening. It was nothing she hadn't seen since she was a little girl, which was the reason she usually tried to turn a blind eye to it, but it was...escalating. David confirming what she'd been thinking lately sent ice water trickling down her spine. And the thought of talking about it to someone, a stranger, made her break out in a cold sweat.

"The truth is, you're scaring the hell out of me, Maddie, and I just..."

She cleared her throat, untangling her fingers to lift her linen napkin and smooth it over her lap. "Nothing is wrong with me. So I've been preoccupied lately. All the other weird stuff...hasn't happened in a while." She dropped her gaze as she uttered the lie and took a sip of her water. "I think you're being unfair. I was running late. It doesn't mean I need a doctor or a therapist. So can we just forget it and enjoy ourselves tonight? I promise I'll do better next time."

Maddie got the distinct impression he wanted to slam his fist on the tabletop. His voice bordered on a hiss. She knew if they'd been alone, it would be a roar. "You promise that *every* time." Gathering his composure, he swept a gaze around at the other quietly dining patrons and leaned across the table toward her. "Look, it's not just the fact that you can't be on time to save your life. It's annoying, but I could deal with it. Last weekend when you stayed over..." He broke off and shook his head, his handsome brow furrowed.

Last weekend when I stayed over, what? Did she want to know? No. She didn't.

"Just...stop."

"Maddie—"

"Did I talk in my sleep again? Tell me that much. Is that it?"

"Yeah, you did. Something about someone coming for you. And you screamed, and you damn near beat the hell out of me when I tried to calm you down, and then you just went...catatonic."

"Okay." She concentrated on keeping her breathing steady, placing her palms flat on the pristine white tablecloth. "I don't remember any of that." And he hadn't told her. He'd been up and gone to work by the time she'd awakened, and she'd simply gone home. They'd spoken since only to make these dinner plans, and even then, she realized, he'd been rather subdued on the phone.

She met his worried gaze with her own. "So I guess tonight is about you urging me to get psychiatric help." So much for her fantasy. His idea of how the evening would end probably involved her being carted away in a straitjacket.

"Regardless of what tonight is about, I want you to get help. You're scared too. Don't deny it. You know I'm right."

What did that mean? There was something he wasn't saying. She knew him well enough. He wasn't looking at her, but thumbing the tines of his fork. The silverware caught the soft golden candlelight and glinted. "And?" she prompted.

His brown eyes flickered up at her, and she read everything

right there. Sadness, weariness...resignation.

"Oh my God," she said softly. "You're leaving me."

He sighed. "This wasn't an easy decision to make."

"So this is your parting advice? 'Get your head checked and have a nice life'?"

"No, it's not like that at all."

"Then what's it like?"

"I'll always be here for you."

"Just like you're here for me now?"

"I *have* been here for you, dammit. Don't sit there and try to tell me I haven't. That time you called me freaking out in the middle of the night, didn't I come over, no matter what I had going on the next morning? You keep doing these things and denying there's a problem, and it's got to stop. Something is going on with you. You need to get it straightened out."

"I'll stop it, then," she said, hating herself. She'd hated herself for calling him like that then too. "I won't worry you anymore. I won't even mention anything is—"

"You'll keep on denying it? What if you—what if everything only gets worse? You'll just suffer in silence until you have some sort of breakdown?"

She opened her mouth, but snapped it closed when the waiter came by and asked for their orders. David muttered that they needed a few more minutes, and then they sat in painful silence while quiet conversations went on around them.

She didn't even tell him some of the things she went through, for the very reason that he was leaving her. Because she was afraid he'd think she was losing her mind. He thought she was crazy enough without her having to tell him about all the clocks tonight. That was a new one, though. She still couldn't believe it herself.

21

But there was one thing she had to know. She bit her lip, wanting like hell to keep the question in, but needing to get it out. "If I agreed tonight to do what you ask and talk to someone, would that change your mind?"

Again, he didn't have to reply. David had always been a fairly easy person to read. For some reason, the devastating truth she saw on his face only prompted her to keep talking, to keep hammering the nail into the coffin of their relationship.

"If I'd never had the first freaky thing happen to me since we met, is this about as long as we'd have lasted? Do you love me? Did you ever love me?"

"I care about you very much. I want only the best for you. And the best for you...honey, it isn't me."

"Apparently it's a padded room."

"Don't do that."

"Just admit we'd be sitting here like this eventually, no matter what."

"If it makes you feel better to know that."

She couldn't contain a sharp bark of laughter that turned heads in their direction. David cringed as he noticed the attention. "I don't think better is quite the word I'd use," she said bitterly. "And that was a real shitty, cop-out thing for you to say, just for the record."

In the candlelight, she saw a muscle flex in his jaw. Which meant he was getting really pissed off. "I didn't want to do this here, Madeleine. That wasn't my intention. I didn't even necessarily want to do it tonight."

"Just choosing your moment to drop the ax? Hey, I get it. The sad thing is, I can't even blame you." She shrugged, trying to block out the sound of her blood rushing in her ears. Panic and horror, denial and defensiveness all warred for domination in her brain, leaving no room for rational thought. Snatching her purse off the floor, she flung the strap over her shoulder and stood.

David rose in front of her and stepped into her path, taking her arm. "Don't leave like this. We're here already...we can still have an evening."

A pity date? Or just hanging out as friends? Was he serious? She jerked her arm from his grip. "Take your hand off me before I *show* you psycho right here in front of all these people."

He held up both hands, as if to say he surrendered. As if he truly believed she would go off and have a screaming fit in the middle of the restaurant. The scene around her began to blur, the pinpricks of candlelight in the votive cups becoming starbursts as tears filled her eyes. It wasn't fair that at that moment, he looked more beautiful to her than he ever had. There was a time she'd dreamed of marrying him, having the perfect house, the perfect family. Perfection, at long last. Denied yet again.

"Goodbye, David." She walked past him. He gave her a wide berth.

Chapter Two

From the shadows, Ash watched her. She burst through the front doors of the restaurant and paused, one hand grasping the iron railing, the other flying to her mouth. For a moment, she stood and looked back at the door, then she raced down the steps, putting distance between herself and the establishment as fast as she could. Thunder rumbled overhead.

This could be it, if he wanted it to be. Her fate was in his hands now—it had been all of her life. Given her distraught state, one subtle manipulation of the stoplights and she could get hit by a car as she crossed the street. He could take her that way, or he could walk up to her, stand face-to-face. Look into her eyes and drag her soul out of her body with one touch. He hadn't decided yet. Either way, it would put an end to all these centuries of wanting her. She'd be his at last, for eternity.

So vibrant. Sometimes a soul shined so brightly it was given more than one turn on the earth because of all the good it could do. So pure and good that his kind didn't stand a chance of corrupting it, or even dared to try.

She was one of those old souls. She'd had several cycles. He didn't know how or why she'd been given such a crap deal this time that he'd been able to find a weak spot to worm his way in, nor did he care. All along, he'd known if he just had a little patience, an opportunity like Maxwell Gatlin would finally present itself.

Invisible as the sudden gust of wind from the approaching spring storm, Ash moved up beside her as she stood at the corner, and stared at her profile. It could have come from a delicate eighteenth century cameo. Silent tears streamed down her cheeks. A shiver racked her and she rubbed her bare arms, almost as if she sensed his presence there...and perhaps she did. She paid the tears no heed, not bothering to wipe them or hide them from other pedestrians. Someone asked her if she was okay; she dismissed the question with a curt nod. The light changed, and she stepped off the curb into the street.

No. Not this way. He didn't understand it himself, but she held such fascination for him, he was content to simply follow her. Watch her. Bide his time until she was ripe for plucking. How and when he would know that, he wasn't sure...but he would.

"So here we are again. When do you plan to take her?"

The crystal clear voice sounded at his back just as a deluge fell from the sky. Dammit. He was currently invisible to the humans, so if someone was speaking to him, that only meant...

He turned and squinted at the blindingly white figure standing behind him. Robes, wings, faint halo, the whole bit— all of it completely unaffected by the sheets of rain sweeping down from the sky. The entire angelic getup was so melodramatic, it always made him smirk. "I was wondering when you might decide to show up."

The angel's gaze followed Madeleine's progression across the street, sadness glinting in the blue depths of his eyes. Ash never could remember their damned names. He never uttered them anyway, so it made no difference.

Ash turned his back on the winged being, summarily dismissing him. "You're wasting your time with this one. I've been waiting eons for this, as you know, and *nothing* is going to deter me. So, save your breath. And your prayers. Don't even think about seeking outside assistance. She's mine."

"There isn't one thing that could persuade you to—"

"No. Not one, not one million. Not for all the stars in the universe would I trade her."

The angel huffed. "At least give her more time."

"For what? For you to slink around and try to sabotage me? I'm afraid your appearance has only made me realize I'd better act fast. Perhaps tonight...as she sleeps. I'll simply rip her soul out, take her home. Show her what she's been missing all these centuries."

"She has done nothing to deserve this. I suppose telling you how disgusting you are..."

"Makes no fucking difference whatsoever. Fly away, now." He set out across the street himself, following Madeleine's hurried steps before she could round the corner up ahead.

"This won't be the last you see of me, demon."

"You'll be too late."

"I doubt that."

When Ash turned to inquire what the angel meant by that pompous, all-too-knowing retort, there was no one behind him. Nimble bastards.

He didn't have time to puzzle over it. Madeleine's heels were clicking away toward the parking garage. Well, he'd show that haloed freak. He'd take her right now.

He caught up behind her as she entered the structure, lured by her delicate lavender scent, captivated by the way her gleaming dark hair clung damply to her shoulders. Her dress was a silky black sheath that accentuated every curve—even more so now that it was soaking wet. Her pale calves were full and lush, and he had the sudden vision of wrapping his hands around her slim ankles and pulling them wide apart. Sliding his hands over the fine-grained flesh while she writhed and begged him to hurry and...

There was a snap, and suddenly Madeleine pitched to the right with a gasp, one arm flailing out to break the fall that was inevitable. It would be too little, too late.

He had no idea why he did it. Later, he would curse himself. Without thinking, without hesitation, Ash dropped his shields and dove, catching her mere inches before her head could hit the curb. She struggled in his grasp and turned to look up at him in shock.

Thunder cracked overhead. Clear blue eyes, wide and fearful and crystalline with tears, met his for the first time.

Shit.

That fucking angel had it right, after all.

Chapter Three

"Oh my God," she gasped, trying to help the stranger as he lifted her and stood her back on her feet. "I'm so sorry. My...the heel of my shoe broke." She bent over and lifted the ruined shoe, inspecting it with a trembling sigh. "That's the perfect ending to a shitty night."

"Sorry to hear," he said, but there was an ironic edge in his voice that didn't sound sorry at all.

"It's no big deal, I guess. I hardly ever wear them." Maddie placed a hand to her chest, trying to coax her racing heart into a slower rhythm. If he hadn't caught her...

"Are you all right?"

She nodded, then tilted her head and inspected her savior. He had black hair, pale skin. Dressed in what appeared to be black jeans and a similarly colored shirt. But how the hell had he caught her? He must have been right on her heels. The thought turned her blood to ice water. She hadn't even heard him, and there was no one around...

He just stood there, watching her. There was something disconcerting about the steady way his gaze rested on her, pulled her in. For a moment, it seemed a struggle to fill her lungs.

Suddenly she became aware that she must look a mess— hair wet, makeup streaked, clothes in disarray. One foot bare.

Something about that darkly intense, heated stare made her want to cross her arms over her breasts, but she resisted the urge. She wasn't showing much cleavage. But beneath her slinky dress and slinkier bra—she'd hoped she might get lucky tonight, after all—her nipples were tightening to stiff little peaks.

"Where did you come from?" she asked, when it appeared he wasn't going to say anything else. Trying to keep her attention away from him, she leaned down to pull off her other shoe and stood on her bare feet. Her soles breathed a sigh of intense relief.

He shrugged broad shoulders. "I was right behind you, heading to my car. I almost tripped over you. You should really buy higher quality shoes, you know. You could have killed me." His mouth lifted in a smirk. Little by little, she'd begun to notice things...like the fact that it was a very nice mouth. His eyebrows were straight and set low over deep, mysterious eyes. The ends of his hair brushed his neck in just the right place.

"A man who encourages shoe buying? Awesome. I might have just hit the jackpot." Well. That had sounded like nothing but a freaking come-on. She wanted to kick herself.

The smirk broke into a very white smile that crinkled his eyes perfectly, and she found herself relaxing a bit and returning it. *Hey, don't get too comfy. Ted Bundy was handsome and charming too.* There was definitely a hint of wickedness behind that smile.

And given the way her luck was running lately...

"Well, um...I don't mean to appear ungrateful, but I have to be going. Thank you for...saving me." She ended on a nervous laugh. The words seemed pitifully inadequate to her own ears. Her skull would have cracked like a melon on that concrete. A fine tremor still worked through most of her muscles, and she hoped she could take a single step without falling flat on her face.

"Aside from the death of a shoe, what's been so bad about your night?" he asked, seeming to utterly ignore what she'd just said. His voice was laced with genuine curiosity, so she didn't mind so much. A hot guy wanted to chat with her. After the rejection she'd just been dealt, it felt pretty good.

Just then a car zoomed past, making her jump. He was waiting for an answer.

"Oh, I don't want to dump all my problems on you."

"What a shame. I'm such a good listener."

Now *that* had sounded like a definite come-on. His voice was as extraordinary as the rest of him, deep and rich with an accent she couldn't trace. She'd never heard that lilt before in her life, but it made her want to ask him to speak. To not stop speaking. And if he could be enticed, to speak into her ear. Preferably while doing unspeakable things to her body.

Whoa, girl. Her previous relationship wasn't even cold in the grave, and five seconds ago she'd been preparing for fight-or-flight. What was she thinking?

You're thinking about taking a total stranger home and screwing his brains out. You're thinking about revenge, about showing David that someone else can want you. Besides, would this guy really have bothered to catch you if he wanted to hurt you?

Well...no. Just no. She wasn't that girl. She'd never had a one-night stand in her life. Sex had always been within the confines of a meaningful relationship.

Uh-huh. And how's that working out for you?

Not a damn bit. It was a sad truth. Her relationships, much like her life, had been one disaster after another—so could she say any of them had been meaningful? How would it even be possible to screw up her love life any more than it was already?

But she wasn't in the headspace to invite a total stranger back to her place, no matter how hot he was. Delia and her other friends could do things like that, but Maddie knew herself. She had a bad habit of falling for the wrong guys, and sex only exacerbated things. It was one more reason David's dumping her hurt so much—he'd probably been the most stable, dependable boyfriend she'd ever had. She'd forced herself to take things slowly and let their relationship progress with as few games as possible, not wanting to sabotage a good thing. Now he thought she was nuts, and he'd never loved her. So even that hadn't worked.

Nothing worked.

Frustration burned hot and bright in her chest, and she stared at her rescuer. If nothing she'd ever done worked, then maybe the one thing she hadn't tried...well, it would at least be a hell of a lot of fun.

"Maddie?"

She cringed at the unwelcome voice. David. Wonderful. Frowning at the intrusion, she straightened the shoulder of her dress and shot a glare at her newest ex. "What?"

His gaze raked her over, taking in her broken shoe, her destroyed makeup and drenched hair. "Are you all right?"

Damn, that was the most often asked question of their relationship, and she hadn't even realized it until that moment. She'd heard it when she woke up screaming at night. When she saw weird things out of the corner of her eye or in the mirror. When utterly unexplainable crap happened to her, like tonight. A large chunk of their time together had been about him seeing to her well-being—and lecturing her—but now he had seen everything the job entailed and he didn't want it full time. She couldn't blame him, but she *wanted* to. For a moment, she felt a pang of sympathy for him. The pain of her predicament quickly gnawed it away.

"You know what, David? I'm not all right. You're so big on me not denying my problems, so there you go. I'm really not all right at the moment. Does that make you feel *better*? Am I making strides?"

"You know what, Madeleine? To hell with you."

Maybe she deserved that, but the anger in his tone left her stricken nonetheless. And mortified, too, but her new friend didn't look very interested in the squabble. He only looked interested in her. In her reaction. Or she was completely misreading things and he wanted to bolt. That was always a possibility. But whatever intrigue he'd piqued in her was doused as if by a splash of cold water, replaced with the slow boil of outrage toward David.

"Please leave," she said quietly.

He didn't reply, just hitched up his jacket and cast an odd look at the dark man who hadn't seemed to take his eyes off Maddie since the interruption. For a moment, she thought David was going to say something to him—warn him off the crazy lady, maybe?—but he didn't. He only walked away.

"Well," she said after David's footsteps faded. It had been disconcerting to meet the guy's gaze before, but now it seemed downright impossible given the embarrassment of the situation. "You just witnessed one of the low points of my existence, and I don't even know your name."

"Call me Ash." The voice was still quiet, controlled. Yet somehow very confident.

Ash. Oh, wow. She liked it. A lot. She imagined saying it in the throes of ecstasy and her heart fluttered like a bird desperate to flee its cage. Could she really do this?

"I'm Madeleine. Maddie. Or I guess you could call me Mad. Damned mad. Whichever you prefer." She shook her head at the idiocy of the joke, but what could she do? Her brain was misfiring.

He chuckled. "Well, Madeleine. I hope your evening improves."

It could. You could help. Unfortunately, his words had sounded like the beginning of a farewell. What had she expected? She'd known from the moment the thought first entered her head that it was impossible. There was absolutely no reason for disappointment to crush her.

Night terrors and one-night stands did not mix.

She bit her lip as tears threatened again, but she managed to push them back where they belonged. David was right, and she knew it. This was becoming incapacitating. It was interfering with her life. She needed help. Maybe she needed a padded room after all.

"I'm sure it will," she said, ignoring the tremor in her words and hoping he would too. "Thanks again for helping me. Good night."

He gave only a slight nod, and she walked away. Now that he was out of her sight, she could...*breathe* again. In fact, she hadn't realized just how weird he'd made her feel until she was away from him. The hairs at her nape settled. Her lungs filled with rush after rush of oxygen, expanding as if they'd been collapsed or in a vise grip for the past few minutes. Finally her mind began to clear somewhat. All that was left in it was despair, a sprawling wasteland of it.

Her yellow Jeep came into view, and she climbed in and sat. Laid her head back, let a few more tears squeeze their way out from between her closed eyelids.

She and David had been together for several months, not

long in the grand scheme of things, but for some reason this felt like being back at square one. Which made no sense. She'd been alone far longer than she'd been with him; she was used to being alone. It was what she was good at. Her mom had bounced from one rehab to another, one county jail to another, until an overdose finally did her in when Maddie was ten. Maddie had been shuffled among aunts and uncles and grandparents from the time she was a baby, never really connecting with any of them. Never really wanting to.

It was almost as if she didn't belong here. She didn't know where she belonged. Or who she belonged to.

At the last thought, she lifted her head and stared at the blank concrete wall beyond the Jeep's front end, feeling the prickle at the back of her neck again. It wasn't the first time she'd felt as if someone, *something*, had a hold on her. Something had to be responsible for all the weirdness in her life.

Or maybe it was just wishful thinking. Because if something was responsible, there was always the possibility it could be dealt with. Banished. And then everything would be okay.

Maybe she needed a freaking exorcism. David had laughingly said it one night, but now she wondered if he'd been serious. That was probably what they would do to her if this were a horror movie.

Nah, David only believed in what he could see. He saw her slowly losing her mind, that was all.

Sighing, she put her head back again. She didn't want to go home. She couldn't face it. Maybe Delia was home from work by now, if she hadn't hit a bar or club on the way. But she didn't want to burden her best friend with her screaming night terrors, either.

The stranger she'd just met...his face floated through her mind. Maybe being alone tonight would be far worse than any embarrassment she might feel if she freaked out in front of someone. A little panicked by the realization, she snatched her cell phone from her purse and dialed Delia, only to get her voicemail. So much for that. Delia was cute and single and enjoyed an impressive sex life that left Maddie amazed and not a little envious. If Delia were here now, she would tell her to run back out there, tackle Mystery Man, and take him home for a therapeutic sex marathon. She probably would have suggested doing this in front of David, if at all possible. But then, her friend didn't take anything seriously. Maddie didn't talk to her very often about her real issues.

Damn. That was it, then. Delia was probably shaking her ass on the dance floor and the mystery man was most likely long gone by now—as if she'd ever have the courage to go look for him to proposition him. Especially since she'd begun second-guessing the signals she'd been reading from him. Sighing, she put the key in the ignition, turned it, and...nothing. The silence of the engine almost seemed to mock her.

"You have *got* to be fucking kidding me."

Chapter Four

He was out of his damned mind. It was the only explanation for why she still drew breath. At any moment, he could have reaped what was his, and yet something in her pleading blue eyes had stopped him cold in his tracks.

She was miserable...well, yes, that was mostly his own doing, and no doubt simply side effects of his claim on her soul. He'd sensed it the moment he touched her, felt every iota of her torment swirl right through him. Glimpsed the pain her former lover had just caused. For that alone, he'd wanted to rip *that* one's soul out. Unfortunately, the man wasn't tainted enough, or the temptation might have been too much to bear.

He'd remained homed in on her, fascinated with the play of emotions across her face, across her thoughts. They were clearer with physical contact, but even from a distance, he'd been able to catch traces of her anger and frustration.

Well, he'd done his job, hadn't he? She'd been sent back to earth time and again for her strength, her goodness and her compassion. He'd broken her down, taken all of that away from her from the time she was an infant. Now she was desperate. She was weak and afraid. He should have been rejoicing over his success, laughing about stealing away and corrupting one of Heaven's favorites. He might even climb the ranks over this one.

If he'd get off his ass and take her, already.

Funny how he was contemplating greatness while he felt like some randy incubus whenever she looked at him with those eyes that were seeking answers for her predicament from somewhere, anywhere. Little did she know she'd found the only being who could give them to her.

He watched from the shadows of the cavernous structure where her vehicle was parked. As she'd slid inside the car, her dress had slithered up one pale thigh, leaving almost her entire leg bared down to the dainty unshod foot. His mouth had watered. His cock had pulsed. It was doing so now, a pleasurable ache that was directly responsible for the idiotic decision to disable her car's engine with a quick blast of his dark magic. To keep her here, to probe her mind and heart some more. To test the silvery threads of desire he'd felt within her roiling emotions, to touch her again.

She'd been so soft, and it wasn't often he felt that particular tactile pleasure. His world was hard and black and scorched, the most forsaken, desolate wasteland anyone could envision. It was home, but a few more brushes of that cool, silken skin and he might grow attached to the topside world. It was a risk he was willing to take.

He approached the side of her boxy yellow car and peered inside. She'd crossed her arms over the steering wheel and was draped over them, her shoulders shuddering. Sobbing. Her hair cascaded over her back and arms, a heavy curtain of silk.

She might tell him to leave her at this point. He might only frighten her. Nonetheless, he lifted one hand and tapped on the window.

Her head jerked up and her eyes met his, widening slightly as their gazes connected through the glass. She made a quick effort to duck and swipe at her cheeks before popping open the car door. "Um, hi." Her voice was raw and husky with tears.

Despite her efforts, dampness clung to her cheeks, and a stray hair caught in the moisture. He longed to brush it away.

"Are you having some trouble?"

Her laugh was without humor. .it was actually one of the most despairing sounds he'd ever heard, and that was saying a lot. "If you only knew what a loaded question that was."

Oh, he did know. "I can help. Maddie."

She softened at his adding her name to the offer. He saw it. Her eyes closed briefly, then she shook her head. "No. You can't. No one can. It's not just that my car won't start, it's...it's everything." Her lips twisted in bitterness. "Every fucking thing."

"He doesn't deserve you." *But aren't you one to talk?*

She made a breathless sound as her gaze darted up to his again, those luscious pink lips parting with surprise. "You don't know anything about me. How can you say that?"

Deciding to risk shattering the fragility of the moment, he lifted his fingers to gently grasp her chin. "I don't have to know you. I have eyes." And he let those eyes wander down to where the bodice of her dress cradled her full breasts, to where the skirt dipped between her thighs. Beautiful. Her figure was lush, curvaceous, just beckoning his hands to chart the dips and swells. His thumb stroked her cheek, where the skin looked like porcelain but felt like satin. It couldn't be his imagination that she was leaning into his touch.

He would have her throughout eternity. But she wouldn't be as she was now, alive and still vibrant despite all he'd taken from her. He wanted a taste of her now, the sweetness of her flesh, the salt of her tears. He wanted to breathe deep the musky fragrance blooming even now from her sex.

Her lips were trembling. "I...do I know you somehow? Have we met before?"

38

Interesting. She never would have seen him, but she most likely would have sensed him near her. She might recognize his presence, know by instinct that he was familiar to her. He allowed a reassuring smile. "Maybe we knew each other in another life."

She wet her lips, staring at his own now. "This is so not me."

"What's that?"

"I don't know you."

"I thought we just established that you did, somehow."

That gained him a tiny smile. "You know what I mean."

"I think I do. You don't know me, and yet..." His finger slid down the curve of her neck, over the persistent throb of her pulse. Delicate muscles tensed beneath his touch. He could now read every turbulent emotion as clearly as if it were his own. What would that feel like if he were buried to the hilt inside her? To feel those emotions crest as she came apart around him? "You want to. You can't explain why. You wonder if it's such a bad thing that you want to let go just once in your life."

His finger reached the neckline of her dress. Her eyes closed, her breath held, as she fell under a spell he wasn't even bothering to weave...at least not by any magical means. She sat very still, captive by his intuitive words alone. "And it's all right. I'm here to tell you that it doesn't matter, not for you. Nothing matters. There's no one to impress anymore, no one to judge you."

"What if I judge myself?"

"Guilt is so useless."

"I think you might be a very bad influence."

Ash traced his finger just inside the edge of her dress. "I

think you should let me be. Take me home with you."

Maddie's eyes opened and she drew a deep breath. She gave a meaningful nod toward the front end of her vehicle. "I hope your ride is nearby."

For a moment he held her gaze, drinking in the molten blue of her eyes. A pretty blush spread up her cheeks, and she made no move to push his hand away. He made no move to test her further. He knew he'd won.

Giving her a crooked grin, he leaned into her car, reached across the steering column and turned the key. The engine purred to life. Maddie gasped.

"What the...? A few minutes ago it was totally dead. How did you do that?"

He stood straight and shrugged with feigned aw-shucks innocence. "I guess I have the magic touch."

She gripped the wheel so tight her knuckles ached, but in the face of the throb in other parts of Maddie's body, her knuckles were the least of her worries.

More than once, she'd asked herself what she was doing. The answer had never really come. Her mind was a humming blank, her body one big raw nerve. From the moment he'd touched her and she went up in flames, there'd simply been no turning back. Crazy? Yes, clearly she'd gone crazy. That was established. She might as well revel in it.

I guess I have the magic touch.

She knew from the pure male cockiness in that comment he hadn't been talking about touching cars. Oh God. She might just be crazy *and* in for the night of her life. The trail of fire he'd left on her skin with just his fingertip still burned. Her entire

40

body thrummed. By the time they reached her apartment, she'd be wound so tight she'd fly apart the moment he put a hand on her.

Well, those magical hands were now resting casually on his jean-clad thighs in her passenger seat. He was quiet, and occasionally she glanced over to watch the passing streetlights intermittently bathe his features with their dingy glow. Every time she looked away from him, she almost convinced herself he wasn't that good-looking. Only to glance over and feel that sweet shock to her senses yet again. His was a face she could spend hours looking at, exploring with her fingertips, memorizing.

Ordinarily silence felt awkward to her, especially when she was one-on-one with someone she'd just met. She always felt compelled to fill it with something. Anything. Not so now. This silence didn't feel awkward—it felt like the calm before a storm, the tense moments spent knowing that something was out there, something huge. Dangerous and intense and raging. But she wasn't afraid, not in the sense that she feared for her safety. She was ready to get tossed on those waves.

"Here we are," she said, hitting the blinker as her heart lodged at the base of her throat. She'd meant for the statement to come out bright, cheerful. It came out like she'd just reached the location of her impending execution.

Maybe it was that, in a sense. She'd left her apartment knowing herself, but it was like she was coming home not only with a stranger, but a stranger herself. The old Maddie, dead and gone. As she turned off the rain-slick street into the parking lot, the dark bulk of her building looked somehow sinister, foreign. Her heart kicked its way out of her throat and began rattling like mad in her chest.

What is wrong with me?

She was no stranger to sinister thoughts, strange forebodings or outright panic attacks. But all three didn't usually assault her at once. And some asshole had taken her usual parking space. She gnashed her teeth as she found another and nudged her Jeep in, then she sat, concentrating on filling her lungs one breath at a time. A fine tremor shook her hands that she hoped he didn't notice. She didn't think she could tolerate one more person tonight who thought she was about to spaz out.

"What's wrong?" he asked. "Second thoughts?"

Was that it? Did she know deep down this was the absolute wrong choice, even though there hadn't seemed to be any *choice* at all?

Then, something incredible happened. He reached over and put his hand on her back. And all the swirling negativity in her thoughts came apart and dissipated, like the storm in her earlier analogy running out of steam. It didn't leave clear skies in its wake, but it did cease its destructive, pummeling onslaught.

His fingers slipped down her spine, carefully tracing each tiny outward curve and subsequent indentation. Scores of chill bumps skittered down her arms, but there was nothing unpleasant about it. "It's all right," he said soothingly.

"My boyfriend broke up with me tonight," she blurted.

"I surmised."

"*Tonight.* Right before I met you, literally not ten minutes earlier. Now here I am with you, and I'm not saying I don't want to be, but..."

"This isn't you," he finished, throwing her earlier words in the parking garage back at her.

"It's so not. And I swear to God I'm not just saying that."

"Why do you think I need convincing?"

"Well..." She closed her eyes as his fingers began the sensuous journey back up the ladder of her spine. Her mouth went dry and her nipples pebbled. She could feel his heat through her clothes, burning hot. He could've been running a fever. But then, it had become almost uncomfortably hot in the confines of her vehicle, and she didn't think it was from his effect on her. *He's going to burn me alive.*

"Well?" he prompted. "Do you think you have to go through life playing the good girl, the saintly one, the one who has it all together?"

"God, no," she said, dismayed. "I sure don't want to give that impression. That's not me, either."

"Then what's the problem?"

All right, maybe it was time to lay it all out there. Even she might not know what was at the root of all her anguish, but at least she could go into this with a clear conscience, knowing she'd disclosed everything. She met his gaze squarely. "Do you want to know *why* my boyfriend broke up with me tonight?"

Ash shrugged, and his answer surprised her. "Why do I need to? Why does it even matter?" His voice dropped to an intimate timbre that exacerbated the shivers racing under her skin, and he leaned so close she could feel his breath on her ear. "See, you are quite saintly, aren't you? So worried the guy you've brought home to fuck will see some deep...dark...*terrible* secret about you." His fingers crept underneath her hair, to her nape, gently massaging there. She wanted to open her mouth and snap a retort to his crass comment, but all that came out was a groan. How did he weave such a spell? It wasn't only his words, but the mesmeric pitch of his lightly accented voice, the ironic undertones. "Is that it, Madeleine? Do you have a deep, dark, terrible secret? Tell me."

The massaging fingers became firm, biting into the tender flesh under the base of her skull. But it felt good. She couldn't fight his grip when he turned her head to face him. She didn't want to, didn't even try. His mouth was so close to hers his breath stole between her lips. Her own breath was coming in ragged little pants. She could gauge its speed by the erratic fluttering of the curlicue of hair hanging in front of her face, until his other hand pushed it away.

The way he spoke of dark, terrible secrets made all of her angst seem like elementary school stuff. That was how she felt with him suddenly, like a trite child dealing with someone much older, more sophisticated and infinitely more knowledgeable. What that knowledge might entail, she wasn't sure she wanted to find out.

"I don't have any dark secrets," she muttered.

His dark gaze flickered over her features. "Of course you do."

"No, I—"

"Very well, then, tell me why that idiot broke up with you tonight. Tell me what's so bad about you that he couldn't deal with it."

"He thinks I'm crazy." It just burst out. Rolled off her tongue as if it didn't even shame her, though it did. She wanted to fold up and disappear. Now he would probably release her like she had the plague, leap from the car and never look back. When he didn't, she was compelled only to keep talking, pushing him, daring him. "He thinks I need a psychiatrist. I see things. Like...these hollow-eyed dead souls in my mirrors. They reach for me. I dream about stuff I can't even describe to you, stuff that makes me wake up screaming and fighting the empty air. Tonight I somehow lost twenty minutes, like a freaking alien abduction or something. And I really don't know why I'm telling you this—"

"Don't stop."

She found she couldn't. Something about him was drawing it out of her, as if the words themselves were being pulled from the depths of her soul. "He thinks I'm too needy, too clingy. He's an idiot. Oh, *I* need a shrink. *I'm* the weak one. What he doesn't realize is if he saw half the crazy shit I did, he would be in a *padded fucking cell* by now."

"Indeed." It should probably disturb her that a slow grin had spread across his face, but it only enflamed her blood more. Dear God, did he understand her? Did he *get* her? After all these years searching for the one who would, had she found him within the space of an hour?

But this was only a one-time thing. She couldn't afford to lose her heart to a stranger.

"Yet I'm still here," she said softly, getting better control of her vehemence so that she wouldn't end up bursting into tears. "I've made it this far, so I'm doing fine. I'm upset at him but I don't need someone to...to rescue me."

His lips brushed the outer ridge of her ear. "Mmm. Was it a savior you were looking for?"

She sucked in a breath at his ministrations, especially when those lips parted and trailed lower, to her neck. Her pussy ached so hard she squeezed her thighs together, trying to assuage the building demand. "I...might have been. Whether I wanted to admit it or not."

Ash's hand dropped to her leg. The entire appendage jumped at the touch, and by reflex her own hand flew down to grasp his. The sudden movement only assisted his hand in slipping under her dress, his hot fingers curling around her rigid muscle. "Maybe tonight I can fill that capacity," he murmured.

All she knew was that she wanted him to fill *something*.

"Maybe tonight, Madeleine, we can do what we can to save each other."

Any remaining resistance inside her broke. She turned her face to his and sought his mouth with hers, finding it even hotter than the rest of him and just the perfect balance between soft and firm. His gentleness surprised her and sent her desire spiraling higher. Her hand abandoned his and she curled her arms around his neck, drawing him closer and leaving him free to explore her body as he wished. She wanted those hands everywhere, anywhere, all over her, right now. His tongue stole between her lips and their mutual groans mingled together, his gruff and strained, hers weak and breathless.

Oh, it was sweet. He tasted like pure heat and sin, and before she realized it, she was tilting her hips toward him, silently inviting his hand to slip farther up her thigh. She spread her legs wider, hoping he'd take the hint. She was wet, burning up, excruciatingly aware of the emptiness throbbing in her sex. "Please touch me," she begged against his lips, when it became apparent he was cruelly content taking his precious time.

He did touch her, but not where she needed him most. His hand moved up to her left breast, cupping its weight as his thumb circled her tightly budded nipple through her dress and bra. God, she needed these clothes *off*. She needed his clothes off. As if he'd read her mind, he abandoned his exploration to grasp the strap of her dress and yank it off her shoulder. He shoved the cup of her strapless bra down and, despite her earlier plea, apprehension overtook lust and she cast a glance out the windshield.

"We should go inside," she said.

His reply was to lean down and kiss the bare swell of her

breast. She couldn't help it; she arched into him, stroking his silky soft hair and murmuring incoherently. His tongue swirled around her nipple and then his lips fastened to it, sucking her so deep and hard it stung. She cried out, the throb in her sex so intense she undulated against the empty air in a vain attempt to ease it.

He obviously had no intention of slaking that need for her. Not in the way she expected. He had her other breast bare now and he divided the attentions of his mouth between them, licking and sucking one, fondling the other, until they were as heavy and aching as her pussy.

Her entire body felt thick and languorous with need, and all she could think about was him plunging into her molten core. How good it would be. *Good* was too weak an adjective, but damned if her brain could be bothered to conjure up another. It would be so good, in fact, the mere thought of those delectable thrusts was enough to drive her over the edge. For the first time in her life, she shuddered with climax while nothing at all touched her between her legs.

When she came to herself, she was sprawled backward, half lying against the door while he leaned over to reach her. She vaguely remembered having cried out words, but couldn't remember for the life of her what she'd said. Her hair was in her face, her skin tingled all over in the aftermath, and Ash looked down at her with dark, lightless eyes. They reflected nothing, not even the overhead lamps outside. But she guessed, given his angle, they wouldn't.

She stared at him in amazement. "No one's ever done that to me before. I mean, made me come...like that."

"Pity."

Maddie agreed completely. Wow. If he could do that barely touching her, what could he accomplish if he had free rein of her body? She hoped, as he withdrew to his seat and she set about fixing her clothes, that he was about to show her.

Chapter Five

Ash had partaken of the delights of mortal flesh before. Many, many times. But none of them, in all his years, had tasted as sweet as his Madeleine. Whether it was because she'd been his forbidden fruit for so long, or if she was simply different from other human women, he didn't know. Nor did he care.

Madeleine unlocked the door to her apartment and led him inside, flipping on a light as she went. Still it was dim, and she kept her face averted, but that didn't hide the rosy blush lingering in her cheeks from their interlude in her vehicle. He longed to put his lips back to that heated flesh and get another taste. Unwrap her luscious body and revel in it all night.

She wandered in the direction of the kitchen, pushing her dark hair back with one pale hand. "Um, would you like something? A drink, or..."

Ash smiled. The only thing he would like right now was her, wrapped around him. "No." Then, remembering the pitfalls of human courtesy, he hastily added, "Thank you."

"Okay." She exhaled as if she were trying to get a grip on some internal struggle. Her gaze met his for a moment, then she bit her lip and turned away. "I'm going to have a glass of wine, if you don't mind."

Why would he? The flavor would linger on her kisses. While

she entered her kitchen, he looked around her living space. He'd seen it before, but there was something bizarre about standing here while she was completely aware of his presence. Oddly, he felt even more like an intruder than when he was invisible to her.

It was small and sparse, but tidy, with little flashes of her personality here and there to cover the imperfections. Colorful pillows to hide a few worn patches on the couch, flowers in oddly shaped vases to cover scratches on the end tables. Books, books and more books. Her main indulgence. They lined shelves, rested in a couple of small stacks on the coffee table. He could picture her curled in the corner of her big, cushy couch, her reading glasses perched on her nose as she escaped into another world. He'd seen her do it many times.

But he wasn't a voyeur—he just liked to peek in at times and watch her do mundane things. Wash her dishes. Vacuum her carpet. Read her books. Most human activity fascinated him, if only because many of them went about their unimportant lives ensconced in their safe little bubbles, blissfully ignorant that they were sitting ducks for him and his kind.

But Madeleine fascinated him even more. She struggled through the life others took for granted knowing full well there was a shadow hovering over her, and yet she soldiered on. She *bothered* to vacuum her carpet and read her books. She was brave enough to try to have relationships. He'd seen others under contract refuse to leave their beds, their lives reduced to nothing but terror. The more they let the fear take over, the more it took from them. Until there was nothing left.

Then again, most of them knew exactly what they'd done, and what was coming for them. Madeleine did not.

It was enough to give him a pang of disgust for the pathetic being who'd given her away so easily. It was also enough to give him a pang of disgust for himself, but he was accustomed to those. There was a cruel injustice about the fact that Gatlin still lived, having been so traumatized by his experience with Ash that he now walked the straight and narrow. That, at least, was a consequence he hadn't seen coming.

Madeleine reentered the room from her kitchen, carrying her wineglass and giving him a wavering smile. "Do you mind if I ask what you do?"

He waved a dismissive hand. "Contracts. It's so dull, I hate to bring the evening down by talking about work. What about you?" But he already knew.

"I waitress, and I work in my friend's indie record store."

"Hmm. And how is it you have a night off from all of that?"

She laughed. "It's rare, but it happens. I have tomorrow night off too, actually. I can't remember the last time I had both Friday and Saturday night off." Her lips closed around the rim of her wineglass and naturally all his thoughts went to where he wanted to see those lips close around his body. The ruby liquid slid toward her mouth, its destination as inevitable as his own. He wanted her. He watched the delicate contractions of her throat muscles as she drank, remembering how she'd come apart in his arms.

Her gaze flickered at him over the rim of the glass, catching the soft light in the room. When she lowered it, she didn't look away, and he didn't want to wait anymore. The time for that was long gone.

He reached her in only a few steps, taking the glass from her trembling fingers and setting it on a nearby end table. "Feel better?" he murmured, following the fall of one silky lock of her hair with his fingertip.

She nodded, and for a moment he thought she wasn't going

51

to speak. "I do. I feel better than I have in a while, actually."

"That's good." His hand reached her neckline and he lifted his other one as well, tracing the straps of her dress before slipping beneath them and urging them off her shoulders. She gasped as her dress fluttered to the floor, making a tiny, sudden movement as if she wanted to cover herself but thought better of it. Considering what they'd just done in her car, it was a little late for modesty, but his lips curled at the gesture anyway.

It was endearing, but completely unnecessary. She stood before him in her bra and panties, neither article of clothing leaving much to the imagination. Black lace barely covered her candy-pink nipples, or hid the sweet juncture of her thighs. She'd worn this for someone else, he knew, but it was that poor bastard's loss. And Ash's very delicious, very enticing gain.

He measured her deep, steady breathing by watching the minute rise and fall of her rounded shoulders, thinking it must be a struggle for her to keep it so slow and rhythmic. He wanted to watch it go out of control with ecstasy again. The thought of pulling the life from this perfect vessel in front of him seemed a sin of the highest order, but that was what he was here for. That was what he wanted. "Has anyone ever told you how exquisite you are?"

Her lashes fluttered as she blinked at him. "Exquisite? No."

"Has anyone ever shown you?"

The question affected her; he'd have to be blind not to see it. For a moment he feared the glimmer in her eye was a welling tear, but her voice held no sign of its presence. "Not really, but that's okay."

It wasn't. These ignorant men in her life—they could have her in a way Ash never could, and not one of them had ever treated her as the treasure she was. They could spend a lifetime with her, form an unbreakable bond based on trust and honesty, love her every night of their lives until death took them. Ash could have her only by lies and deception and underhandedness. He could have her only by stealing her.

Not *one* of those others had ever made her feel as she did now with only his gaze caressing her flesh. He knew because her emotions were coming through loud and clear. If he'd had a heart, it would be breaking for her.

Quite possibly, it was all his fault. He was the one who'd broken her. She'd never had a chance.

As if some string that had been holding her captive suddenly snapped, she surged forward and caught his face between her hands, caught his lips with her own. Blind lust ripped through him, blazed a trail through the cold wasteland of his soul, and he met her on the same plane of hunger and desperation. Her soft body pressed tight to his, her lavender-tinged scent swirled in his mind. Her warmth suffused him.

Gripping her ass, he lifted her against him and headed instinctively to her bedroom, every step torture as she ground against the hard ridge of his cock—his hard-on hadn't abated since the parking garage and now it bordered on painful. He almost missed the door and barely avoided slamming her into the frame. She giggled as he cleared it, her mouth unwilling to leave his. A little squeal escaped her as he tumbled them both onto the bed.

He paused and stared down at her, smoothing the hair back from her forehead. Her face was cast half in shadow and half in the light filtering in from the window. Split in two, light and dark. Much like her soul. As he watched, her swollen lips parted and the tip of her tongue swept the bottom. Ah, she was trying to kill him. He was nestled in the cradle of her thighs, and every tiny movement of her hips sent lightning through his system. It might only be his imagination, but he could swear he felt the damp heat of her even through his jeans.

"This isn't fair," she whispered, her hands creeping under his shirt. "I'm damn near naked and you're not."

"It's a problem," he agreed, lifting so that he knelt between her thighs. Never taking his gaze from hers, he began unbuttoning his shirt. She watched the progress of his hands, the pulse jumping at the base of her throat. He thought he could practically hear it drumming in his ears. No sooner had he completed his task than she sat up and pressed her soft lips to his stomach, just above the edge of his jeans.

His muscles jumped at the contact, tensing when her wet little tongue flickered against his flesh. A growl caught in his throat as he flung the shirt the rest of the way off; his hands sank into her hair hard enough to hurt, but she didn't utter a single whimper. Instead, her nimble fingers attacked the button of his jeans, and he grasped the opportunity to reach behind her and unhook the cursed bra that kept her hidden from his sight. She tore it away and yanked his jeans down his thighs, freeing his cock and giving a mew of appreciation.

Bliss engulfed him whole. It was her hands on him, wrapping lovingly around his girth, her warm breath tickling across the head. But if she laid those pretty, wet lips on him at this point, he would lose his last tenuous grip on control.

He grasped the sides of her head, wrenching it upward so she could receive his kiss. And receive it she did, every bit as wild as he was, their tongues dueling and teeth nipping. He propelled her backward again, catching his weight on his elbows so as not to crush her.

"Ash, touch me," she whispered, undulating her hips so that she rubbed against his erection. Only one tiny barrier existed between them now, and it was sweet torture. Now he could for damn sure feel how wet she was; the panel of her lacy black panties was drenched and he deliberately stroked the head of his dick over it as she arched against him. *"Please.* I can't wait any longer."

Oh, she had no idea about *waiting.* About agony. He wasn't too keen on teaching her about them at the moment, either. He'd had enough of both.

She gasped into his mouth as her panties gave with one wrenching pull, the elastic no doubt biting into her flesh as it snapped. The scent of her need swirled in his head, intoxicating him, drawing his balls up tight. Her hands skated up and down his back, her nails lightly scoring his flesh. She lifted her hips, causing his shaft to graze her wet clit, and the sound she made in his ear was nearly his undoing. Hard little teeth clamped onto his earlobe, driving a curse from his lips.

By the Dark Lord, but he'd never seen a more perfect image of unhinged lust. He reached between them and slipped his fingers between her legs. She sighed and relaxed beneath him as if he'd soothed her, as if he'd eased some raging discomfort for her. Her legs fell farther apart, giving him more room to explore the damp, delicate tissues, the tight little bud he'd later like to spend an hour licking and sucking until she screamed or begged him to stop. One little tilt of her hips and his fingertip slid lower, seeking and finding the tight entrance to her body. Madeleine gave a frantic little jerk as he breached it, her hands clenching on his shoulders even as the muscles of her inner walls fluttered around his finger. Holding him, pulling him in, demanding more.

It was on the tip of his tongue to whisper to her how long he'd wanted her. But that would prove catastrophic. She wouldn't understand. Likely, she never would. This was his one and only opportunity to have Madeleine, and he wouldn't have given it up for all the souls in the world.

He squeezed another finger inside her and stroked, thrust slowly in and out, building her need as her little cries lilted into the silence of her bedroom. Her hips found his rhythm and met it, rolling with it, her pussy so wet, so soft...

"Demon! Demon!" a weird voice croaked from the corner of the room.

What the *fuck*. Ash cranked his head around, lifting his hand from Madeleine's warmth as she gave a curse that was half amusement, half frustration.

Who'd let the goblins out? And why were the little bastards set on sabotaging him? As he scanned the corner of the room, all he could see was what looked like a black sheet draped over a large, oddly shaped object.

"Sorry," Maddie said. "I was hoping he'd stay asleep."

"What the hell is that?"

"My parrot. He's just introducing himself."

"Demon! Demon!" the bird insisted.

"Introdu—" He snapped his mouth shut, utter confusion momentarily robbing him of coherent thought. "That's his *name*?"

"Yeah," she said. "Well-earned, I promise you."

"You have a bird named Demon."

"Mm-hmm. I can't take credit for it though. The guy I got him from had already named him that."

Wild wing-flapping ensued under the black cover. "Demon! Demon! Mum's the word!"

Well, thank hellfire for small favors. Ash shook his head at this new development, and then the absolute absurdity of the situation hit him full force and something incredible happened, something that hadn't happened in a very, very long time.

He laughed. Not in malice, or wicked glee at the suffering

he'd inflicted on another, but true, genuine laughter. Madeleine joined in, her fingers sinking through his hair as his head dropped to her naked shoulder.

"Talk about a mood-killer, huh?" she said, shuddering with her own giggles. "I'm so sorry."

"No, don't apologize. It was just...entirely unexpected."

"I'm sure he just, um...heard my voice and got all excited."

"Understandable. I got pretty excited hearing you too." He nuzzled at her throat, and she tilted her chin back for him. "Now, where was I? Right about...here?" He slid his finger down and drew teasing circles around her nipple. It responded enticingly, drawing up into a hard little peak. He kissed a trail to it, licking and nipping with his teeth.

"That's nice, but I think you were lower than that," she murmured. Then she moaned as he latched on to her nipple, sucking it into his mouth and holding it there mercilessly as his hand trailed downward. His fingertip slid into the tiny dip of her navel.

He released the suction on her breast with an audible little pop. But he couldn't go far away; her hand was holding the back of his head, fisting in his hair. "Here?"

"Lower," she said, her voice throatier and more urgent than it had been moments ago. Her hips were moving again, seeking to grind against him. He abandoned her breasts to move down her body, absorbing her shivers as he settled his shoulders between her thighs. Only then did he allow his finger to slide down, down, and slowly circle her clit.

"Here?" he whispered.

Her thighs jerked. "There's good. Anywhere around there is good."

A chuckle escaped him as he turned his attention to the

vision in front of him. Bare. Delicate. Her moisture glistened in the scant light from the window and enticed him to taste it. Even in the darkness, he could see she was flushed and swollen with her need. She was as soft against his fingers as she looked, and he took his time touching her until his mouth watered for a taste. He slid two fingers into her drenched heat, listening to her breathing go out of control. Just the way he'd wanted. She stretched around the intrusion, so sweet, so accepting. Her own hands came down and found the backs of her knees, pulling her legs farther apart.

"Beautiful," he murmured, drawing his fingers out to their tips before slowly plunging back in again. And again. And again.

"Oh God," she cried. "Oh, yes. Don't stop."

How could he? To show her just how intent he was on not stopping, he leaned forward and closed his lips around her bud. Felt her entire body shudder with the shock of it. Her taste exploded in his mouth, tangy and sweet, and he tongued her as if he meant to lap up every precious drop of her arousal. He curled his fingers inside her, giving her little come-hither motions that brought her ass off the bed, and he caught her there with his free hand, holding her thrusting hips captive. Her hands released her knees and sank into his hair. He liked that, liked holding her fast to him while she clasped him to her, each of them imprisoned by the other's pleasure, completion the only chance for deliverance.

Ash felt it begin, the gripping heat of her pussy rippling around his fingers as the muscles in her thighs pulled tight as bowstrings over his shoulders. So much energy poured off her, so much emotion, and he soaked it up, drank her in and craved more. More of her, her body and soul stripped bare and his for the taking. He held her to his mouth, nibbled and licked and suckled her through it until she collapsed panting and cursing and trembling on the bed.

He crawled up the length of her, glad for the moment her eyes were closed and her face turned away because he had no idea what might be revealed in his expression. There had never been a more beautiful, vulnerable sight. It called to his inner beast, taunted it. Tempted it to run wild. One of her hands was on her forehead and the other fluttered to her chest as she tried to catch her breath, her breasts quivering. The silk of her inner thighs brushed his hips.

He slid his fingers under hers, felt the pounding of her heart beneath her breastbone. So strong. So full of life. Life that was his for the taking. This was how it would begin. His dark energy would gather, pulse through him into her. It would detach her spirit. It would hurt, and he wished he could avoid that, but there was nothing to be done for it. It wouldn't last long, and then she would be his. Forever.

Chapter Six

She'd never been orgasmically challenged, thank God, but that had been one freaking amazing orgasm. Maybe there was something to be said for this love-them-and-leave-them stuff. It sounded ridiculously corny and cliché, but she was still seeing stars. Right there, behind her closed eyelids, they danced and exploded. She was content to watch them for the moment, lest she look at his face and fall so totally and deliriously in love the whole love-them-and-leave-them thing would become a moot point. And that's what she *didn't* want. That was where she always messed up.

His fingers rested on her chest, caressing her over her beating heart. The weight of his hand there made her feel weird, like everything on the inside of her was drawn to it, compelled to answer some summons. A tingling, tickling ache went out to all her limbs, and she frowned, trying to squirm away from the sensation. She was floating too high on a cloud of bliss for any freakiness right now, at least any freakiness that didn't involve sex. Ash, she needed more of Ash. She wasn't done with him yet. Encircling his fingers—incredibly warm fingers, almost burning hot—with her own, she drew his hand to her mouth, the weird ache dissipating as if it had never been as she kissed one of his fingertips. Flickered her tongue against it, parted her lips and drew it inside. Only when he groaned did she open her eyes and look up at him.

His face was drawn, his brow furrowed, almost as if he were in pain rather than the throes of pleasure. His eyes were closed, sensual lips parted.

Was it weird of her that she didn't think she'd ever felt more *appreciative* in her entire life? Tonight she should be drowning her sorrows in chocolate and liquor. If not for him, she would have been. She would have ridden the woe-is-me train straight through until the dawn, and then she would have to face tomorrow alone.

She would still have to face it alone, but at least she would have the glow of great sex around her. At least she would know the night before she'd had someone to laugh with, to make her feel good. It was all thanks to him. And she'd yet to return the favor. The hard length of him against her belly didn't let her forget it. He was as hot and heavy as a brand lying against her.

His eyes opened and his gaze met hers. Stole her breath. Not because of any sappy romance in the dark depths, but the promise of passion so wild and consuming she didn't know if she'd ever be the same again. He almost...almost scared her, with that look. Scared her and tempted her. Reminded her of that moment in her Jeep when she'd felt as if a storm was coming. It was here now, poised on the brink of unleashing its fury all over her.

Words crowded in her throat. She didn't know which to utter. *Fuck me, take me, hurt me, oh, God, make me forget my life, make me not care if tomorrow comes...*

All she said was his name, and it was enough.

He fell on her like she was the oasis and he the parched desert traveler, his hand winding around behind her head and lifting her into his kiss. She opened to him, lips and legs parting for him to fit even closer to her. His tongue invaded her mouth as surely as she wished his cock would invade the hot need

61

throbbing in her core.

"Condom," she gasped against his lips, and heard his low answering growl. It sounded more like frustration than anything else. She understood that totally, but... "I have some, if you don't. In the drawer right there..."

Never mind. She didn't have time to wait for him to rummage around in an unfamiliar space looking for them. She reached over herself and he lifted to allow her. Mercifully, she found a little packet, ripped it with her teeth and reached between them. "Come here, baby." Ordinarily she loved to watch a man do this, watch his hands stroke efficiently over himself as he rolled it down, but again, she didn't have time to savor any moments here. If she didn't get him inside her soon...

Oh, *damn*, he was gorgeous. Long and thicker than she'd even hoped, the dusky flared head already leaking a pearly drop she longed to lick from him. He was going to feel so good she might not make it through this. She might die. End of problems.

She swallowed a hysterical giggle, scarcely believing she was about to get spectacularly laid with a complete stranger. Yeah, it was so not her, but maybe she'd just met another side of herself she hadn't known existed. Maybe they should get better acquainted.

Her task finished, she settled back on the pillows and he followed, stretching out over her. The minor condom speed bump had little effect on their momentum. He kissed her hard and she was lost again, flipping end over end through a maelstrom of lust. The blunt head of him found her entrance, feeling ten times bigger than it had looked, and the death she was anticipating, oh yeah, it was coming for her after all. She nearly came just from the touch of him there, and when he pushed...

The world ended. And began again. He stretched her beyond the point of pain, but so many sensations mingled it was impossible to extract it from the pleasure. Just when she thought he couldn't give her any more, he had more to give her. Her fingernails dug into his shoulders, she caught his hips in a death grip with her thighs.

"So fucking good," he murmured in her ear. She could only sob her agreement. Good, so good, she didn't think anything had ever felt so good. He was burning hot above her, inside her, damn, she melted around him. But he wasn't moving fast enough—he wasn't moving at all—and she needed to *move.*

"Please," she whispered, making a little circle with her hips, the most she could do with him pinning her to the mattress. "Ash, please."

A gruff sound burst from his throat. Slowly, so slowly she wanted to scream, he pulled out inch by inch. Her body clung to him, gripped him, protested his retreat. He withdrew until he was poised at her entrance again, slick with her juices. The aching emptiness he left in his wake seemed to spread out to include all of her, until she was one big vessel waiting to be filled up by him and him alone. It was the singularly most terrifying thought she'd had in a long while, and she didn't know why. When he kissed her and nearly drew tears with his tenderness, she did.

It was going to be damn hard letting go of him. How would she not spend the rest of her life wishing she had *this* every night?

His gaze drew back and found hers. His hips surged. The rhythm he set punished her. So wet now, so easy, she took him all, tossing her head on the pillow as ecstasy devoured her. He knew just how to move, how to twist his hips to hit all her sweet spots, and she bit her lip on cries that would have her neighbors dialing 911, because surely that quiet girl next door was being brutally murdered.

"Madeleine," he groaned, every iota of pleasure she was feeling evident in his voice. She loved how he had the presence of mind to say her whole name; she could barely remember it. He somehow flared even hotter against her. She was liberally slicked with sweat, when he didn't seem to have broken one at all, and hers was as much from the heat he was generating above as the heat he was generating within. She didn't know if she could take much more without combusting.

"So close, I'm so close," she whispered hotly in his ear, as much to encourage him to keep doing it *just like that* as to hurry him along to his own completion. She wanted to come with him. It had never been something she cared about before and it was something that had rarely, if ever, happened. But everything about this had been so perfect she couldn't imagine a better ending than for both of them to fall into bliss together.

She felt the shudders and the tightening of her muscles begin. She couldn't stave it off. It grew inside her, eclipsing her, frightening her with its power. A few more strokes, a few more brushes against her clit, and she'd be there, she'd be...

The building pressure crested and dissolved into rolling waves of mind-numbing pleasure. That storm she'd been waiting for, that fury, blew over her, and she hung on to him as the only anchor in all this wildness. But even in the tumult, she felt his hips jerk away from the smooth, sure rhythm he'd maintained, heard his rough groan in her ear, and knew that she'd gotten her wish. She wasn't alone in the storm.

Time passed, she wasn't sure how much, just that it seemed the night would never end and that was damn fine with her. Ash was the most insatiable lover she'd ever known. When they finally collapsed, exhausted—at least, she was—she'd expected him to announce any moment that he was going to get up and call a cab. She hadn't expected to lie face-to-face with him like this, talking. Talking about nothing and everything, with his fingers trailing lazy linear patterns on her arm.

Was this supposed to be part of the deal? She'd heard Delia talk about her sexual escapades and never had she mentioned the time spent baring your soul to the guy you likely would never see again. But Ash asked her questions about herself, seeming genuinely interested in her answers, even if he wouldn't offer up many of his own. She found, finally, that she couldn't keep quiet about it.

"Why all the interest in me?"

His brows drew together, dark eyes flickering up from where he'd been watching his fingertip trail down her neck. "What's that?"

"Why me? I know I happened to fall into your arms quite literally tonight, but...what made you pursue a pathetically weepy female with obvious baggage?" Her lips twisted with bitterness as a new thought struck, a thought that should've struck long ago—that should've knocked the hell out of her, actually. "Pity?"

"No." The answer was sharp and without hesitation. "Never that. I'm not philanthropic enough for that."

"Well, what, then? I mean...I'm not usually down on myself, but I can't look that damn interesting. I wouldn't take a look at myself and automatically think 'sex strumpet' or anything."

A grin curled his lips. Lips she could stare at all night. Lips she pretty much *had* been staring at all night. "How lucky for us that I did. Even luckier that I was right."

She gasped with mock outrage. "Oh, *really*." They laughed together, but soon as they sobered, she couldn't resist pressing the matter. "I guess that's kind of lame, huh? Questioning your judgment and all."

"Very lame."

"Told you I wasn't very good at this."

"Actually, you only told me this wasn't you, never that you wouldn't be good at it. I found you quite good."

"Gee, thanks."

He just looked at her—God, she couldn't get over how he looked at her. And how something deep in those dark eyes made her feel, crazily enough, as if he knew her. It wasn't the first time the thought had occurred to her.

Her phone buzzed insistently on the nightstand, shattering the spell. She'd forgotten she'd meant to turn the damn thing off a while back, because even though it was after 3:00 a.m., David kept calling and texting her. Ash had kept her too occupied to worry much about it, though. She'd glanced at the display only once when she'd gotten up to go to the bathroom, but she had a pretty good idea he was still the one who was trying to get in touch with her.

Ash was watching her intently. Maybe the blend of her annoyance, guilt and grief was showing on her face. "Your boyfriend?" he asked.

"Ex," she reminded him.

"I don't think he's really all that happy about the ex part."

"He should have thought of that before he strapped himself with it."

"I don't think you're all that happy about it, either."

"Well, naturally...no one likes getting dumped." She walked her fingers up his shoulder. "But I suppose it makes it a whole lot easier when you have someone to help you pick up the pieces."

"Do you love him?"

"Oh. I, um..." Did she? She was upset, sure, and it stung like hell...but was she *heartbroken*? Or was it merely another case of someone she thought she could depend on leaving her? Did she really mourn David, or only what he represented? A normal life, security, stability, maybe a family. She'd always wanted a family. People who could depend on her to help hold them together. No one in her life had been able to do that for her.

He was waiting for her answer. She sure as hell didn't owe him one. But he had that way, that damn way of looking at her that made her certain she was going to answer him all the same. "I cared about him a lot. Maybe I even loved him. Or maybe real, true love was possible, but would only have come later. I don't know."

"Did he ever make you feel like I just did?"

She frowned at him, stunned he would ask such a thing. Especially with that smug, arrogant little tone. Most guys didn't want to hear about their predecessors. But then, he was kind of a strange guy.

Oh, shit. She hoped to God—not for the first time, but for perhaps the most fervent—he wasn't some psycho stalker. His tattoos alone were pretty scary...she hadn't noticed them until he got up to get her a drink earlier, and the sight of them had drawn an audible gasp from her. The thick, elaborate black patterns swirled all the way across his back and down to his butt. She didn't mind a tattoo, but that one had been off-putting. The sheer amount of work and pain that must have gone into it...and what the hell did it mean? She'd asked, once she regained use of her voice, but he just shrugged and said he'd thought it looked cool. Okay. Then he'd come back to bed and made her forget all about it. For the time being.

"I don't really feel like discussing my sex life with David, if it's all the same to you."

He scoffed. "Well, that answers my question. Come on, Madeleine. He was nothing to you. I saw the tears you shed over him and they were a *crime.*"

She looked at him for a moment, then sat up and hugged herself, suddenly unexplainably chilled. "You say that like you know it for a fact."

"I do."

"You can't."

"Everyone leaves you, don't they?"

"*What?*"

"It's a wonder you let anyone close to you at all. You only let me in because you expect that I'll be gone tomorrow. No surprises. No pain. Right? Everyone you just told me about in your life, your mother, grandparents, aunts and uncles...none of them are in your life anymore, are they? You're utterly alone."

Who the hell *was* he, mind-fucking her like this? "What does it matter to you? You *will* be gone tomorrow, so quit trying to head-shrink me. I already had that fight tonight. What are you, a psych student and I'm a fucking experiment for you?"

He leaned up and, to her utter bemusement, skimmed his hands up her bare arms. Her shoulders. Gooseflesh exploded over her skin as if a phantom breath had gusted across it. His hand came to rest over her heart, which leapt toward him as if it wanted to break free and feel the squeeze of his fingers around it. A tiny sound erupted from her throat. She must be seriously disturbed.

"I'm sorry," he whispered, lowering his lips to her shoulder. He trailed a warm path to her neck and, against her better judgment, she found herself leaning her head away to give him easy access. After everything they'd done tonight, she still turned to liquid beneath his touch. "But you intrigue me. So much."

Why? She'd asked him already, but he wouldn't answer. And she wished he would, wished he could tell her something that would make all the madness make sense, all the pieces of her life fall into place.

That was ridiculous. Wasn't it? Still, the idea wouldn't leave her alone.

"Everyone leaves me," she whispered, stunned when the words slipped from her lips. Once they were out, she couldn't build up a dam fast enough to stop the rest. "You're right. But I've learned to deal with it. I've learned to put up walls, to not let anyone get too close."

It had all started with her mother. Sad, that she could pinpoint the moment when things started going out of control in her life—but had there ever been control of any sort? A kid could only be lied to so many times before she began to grow wary and mistrustful. By the time her mother had OD'ed, after years of empty promises and failed attempts to get sober, Maddie had been so removed from her own emotions she could remember looking in that casket and thinking that thin waxy figure inside wasn't anything that had ever been attached to her. It had never loved her or cared about her at all.

She wanted to unload all of that on someone, she realized. Maybe she did need therapy. Or maybe she just needed *this*. Someone to put his arms around her and not question her sanity. To whisper in her ear it was all right. Even if it was only for tonight, the night when she needed it most.

"I'm...sorry, Madeleine, that you were hurt," Ash said, his lips brushing her ear as the words left them. He sounded as if...as if he really meant it, which struck her as odd, because it implied he hadn't meant anything he'd said all night.

"I'll be fine. I always have been," she said, hearing a quake in her voice she hoped he would dispel. Suddenly she wasn't so tired anymore. And there was only one kind of therapy she craved.

Chapter Seven

The nightmare came; she'd known it would. It was never the same dream, but the same undercurrent of darkness ran through them all, like an obscene watermark. She recognized *those* dreams as soon as they began, recognized them, but was powerless to wake herself up or escape until the dream was done with her. By then she always stood at the edge of sanity with hurricane-force winds at her back, pushing her ever closer to the dizzying drop below.

Screaming, she clawed her way from under the sweat-soaked sheets, fighting the hands reaching for her, dead skeletal hands intent on dragging her down and imprisoning her in the earth until she suffocated on black, stinking dirt...she felt it already, filling her throat, and she couldn't *breathe*, couldn't—

Strong hands caught her, even more solid than the ones trying to kill her. She flailed against them, slapping wildly until both her wrists were shackled with fingers that felt like iron bands and pinned down to the bed.

The bed. Not the endless black maw of a waiting grave.

"Madeleine. *Madeleine.* Wake up." There was strength in the voice, an undeniable command she responded to, mind, body and soul.

Her eyes flew open. Her own damp hair streaked her vision,

but above her a face appeared. For one frantic moment it looked as threatening as the ones that had been taunting her since she fell asleep, but then everything came into sharp focus. Her room. The pale blue stain of dawn creeping in from her window. Ash. He was still here; he hadn't left her. Tentatively, he loosened his hold on her wrists, a furrow creasing his brow.

The words burst out before she could stop them, her automatic response to David whenever she'd woken him up in such a way. "I'm sorry!"

He released her, settled next to her and pulled her into his arms. She rested her cheek against his naked chest, inhaled him and wished she could disappear inside him. She wasn't crying—she was always too terrified to cry—but she was shaking all over. His warm solidity against her was the only thing keeping her from flying apart.

"It's all right," he murmured against her hair.

Minutes passed, and true embarrassment began to fill the emptiness left in the wake of panic. She didn't want to lift her head from his chest because she didn't want to face him, didn't want to have to explain. Not that she owed him anything. It was morning, so surely he'd be out the door and out of her life within an hour. Better to just let it go and get back to reality.

Reality would be good. The nightmare still hovered at the fringes of her memory, intruding despite her efforts to hold it at bay. She tried to breathe deeply, slowly, but her lungs refused to cooperate just yet.

Then Ash tilted her chin up and kissed her.

She hadn't expected it, wasn't prepared. She only had time for one fleeting fear about morning breath and then she was swept away.

Nothing was wrong with the way he tasted. It was better than coffee. His lips gently teased hers apart and his tongue slipped between her teeth, the sensual motions reminding her in excruciating detail of the other things he was good at doing with it. His hands cradled her face; his biceps flexed under her hand...a hand that wasn't clenching him in fear any longer, but softening with desire.

How did he do that? How did he chase away all the bad stuff?

"Better now?" he murmured, pulling away only to continue taking little nips at her mouth.

"Mm-hmm," she replied, scarcely recognizing her own voice. She sounded sated, fulfilled...she even felt sleepy again. When she opened her eyes, she saw that the morning was slowly chasing away the last of the shadows in her room. Usually she welcomed it. This particular day, she would like to be able to postpone its arrival, only for a while.

Ash laid her head back down on his chest, stroking her hair. "Go back to sleep."

It sounded divine, but still sent a little sliver of panic through her. "I don't know if I can. The dreams—"

"I'll keep them away."

It was cheesy, romantic nonsense, but something melted around her heart.

She almost believed him.

Delia was late to her own store, as usual. No big deal. It wasn't as if a line was waiting when Maddie unlocked the door and disarmed the security system.

It was almost eleven. She'd had a couple more hours of blessedly dreamless sleep in Ash's arms and then she'd seen him off. It had been...odd, a little awkward, and he'd seemed reluctant to leave, looking at her in a way she found confusing. As if there was something he wanted to do or say before he finally gave up the battle with himself and kissed her goodbye. Nothing had been said about seeing each other again, but of course, he knew where to find her if he wanted.

She knew nothing about him. No phone number, no address...that ball was entirely in his court. She'd be a freaking liar if she said she hoped he wouldn't do something with it. So much for love them and leave them.

Delia bounced in thirty minutes later, bearing a bakery box and Starbucks despite it being nearly noon. She'd probably just rolled out of bed herself. Her shoulder-length black hair wasn't as immaculately tousled as usual, but smooth and flat. Her eyes were covered with oversized sunglasses.

Maddie eyed the box and cocked an eyebrow at her. "I was thinking about *lunch.*"

"Hell, I'll eat all this and whatever you go get. I'm starving." Delia tossed the white box on the counter and flipped it open, attacking the flaky pastry with gusto. She bit into one and her face underwent a shift to orgasmic bliss.

Maddie reached over and pulled Delia's glasses off, tilting her chin up and inspecting her eyes as the other girl chewed and stared back impassively. Clear. "No hangover, then? I'm impressed."

"Nah. I didn't even go out."

"Really? I tried to call you."

"I crashed early."

"What's gotten into you?"

Delia shrugged. Only after she'd demolished a croissant did she sip her coffee and pass Maddie her own. "Did you get me cheese danish?" Maddie asked.

"It's *lunch*time," Delia mimicked, propelling the box toward her. "Of course I did."

"Like I need it." She'd packed on a few extra pounds in the past several months...okay, more than a few. She was a stress eater, and, well, there had been a lot of stress to eat about lately. Two weeks ago, in a fit of rage, she'd tossed her scales in the cabinet under the sink. It was too depressing to watch the numbers climb. "I need to start exercising," she announced suddenly.

Delia almost choked, managed to swallow with an audible gulp. "Jesus, Mad, when would you have time? Sometimes I want to fire you just so you can relax."

"Ha. Don't you dare. I would starve."

"Well, maybe I would feed you every now and then."

"Gee, thanks."

"It's only because I love you. So, how did your date go last night?"

She'd known the question was coming. For the past couple of days she'd been confiding in Delia about her hopes for last night. Breathing deep, she said, "You wouldn't believe me if I told you. You absolutely will not believe it. I mean, I'm glad it's not April Fool's Day, or you'd accuse me of trying to pull one over on you."

Delia's round blue eyes had grown even rounder and seemingly even bluer as Maddie spoke. "What the hell. Did he *propose*?"

"He dumped me."

Delia's jaw dropped. "That bastard! Holy crap! Mad...I mean, holy crap! Why the... what the... Dude, you look pretty awesome for just having been dumped. I mean, you're *glowing*. It doesn't make any sense. With the way you're looking, I was expecting you to flash your fucking new diamond sparkler or something."

"It makes perfect sense once you hear all of it."

"What, did you make up and break up all in one night? Wild make-up sex?"

"I think we can safely say David is out of the picture. There was no wild make-up sex. There was, however, wild sex."

Maddie chanced a look at her friend and burst out laughing. There was no description for the look on Delia's face. She only wished she had a camera to capture it for posterity. Or just to hang on the wall in this place. Plenty of the regulars would get a kick out of it.

"With *who*?"

"Oh God, Dee. This guy. I met this *guy* by some freak accident in the parking garage as I was leaving the restaurant. And he was...wonderful and gorgeous and sexy, and we talked for only a few minutes but...I took him home with me."

"Holy shit! I'm...speechless! And speechless never happens to me."

"I know, right?"

"So, spill. Details, girl."

"Oh, I can't go into all the lurid details. But he was...he was awesome." Maddie practically felt the wistfulness in her own smile as she lifted her coffee to her lips. She glanced at Delia over the cup. Her friend shook her head slowly, still in disbelief.

"Damn. I feel as proud as a...as a mother or something, like my little Maddie is all growed up now."

"Let's not be ridiculous. It happened, and it was good, and it definitely got my mind off things. If nothing else, it showed me there's plenty more out there. David wasn't the be-all, end-all."

"So are you going to see this guy again? Tell me his name,

at least. Maybe I know him if he's from around here."

"I don't think he is. He's got a little bit of an accent, but I can't place it. He didn't talk about himself much...but his name is Ash..." *Damn.* She hadn't even asked his last name. "Um, well, we didn't get that far. But I doubt I'll be seeing him anymore. It was just one of those things, you know?"

"Maddie. To *me* it would be just one of those things. But to you? I don't mean to sound all maternal on you for real, but...are you sure you're okay with this?"

The question sent an odd pang through her. She didn't like how it seemed to curl up and reverberate. Flashes from the night before assaulted her...Ash's hands on her skin, his eyes looking down at her. His hard body, the sound of his voice. For that moment, all of her senses were overwhelmed and she could still feel him deep inside her where she was still tender and aching. She waved her hand, pretending to be absorbed in looking at a couple of CDs stacked on the counter. "I'm fine."

"You obviously like him."

"Well...yeah, of course—for the few hours I spent with him. But so what? I made the decision. I'm a big girl, I can deal with it."

"So what is David's problem?"

Oh no. To tell her that would be to admit what she was going through, what she'd always gone through. What if Delia came to the same conclusion as David? What if *Maddie* was slowly coming to the same conclusion? That was the worst thought of all.

"David...doesn't love me." Hey, it was the truth. The truth underlying it all, actually. "End of story."

"I'm so sorry, hon."

"Yeah, well. You lose some, you lose some." A bitter chuckle escaped.

"Look, there's someone out there for you. I think maybe you should give Mr. Hot Stuff from last night a shot, see if this can go beyond the bedroom. Any man who puts a look like that on a woman's face is worth the chance. Hell, I wish I could find that."

Involuntarily, Maddie lifted a hand to her cheek. Did she really look that different from one night of sex? "I don't really want to see anyone, though. I'm—" She cut off, coming dangerously close to explaining that she was dealing with *so much crap* right now, but she didn't want Delia asking about it.

Sadness settled in her soul. *I don't have one friend I can really talk to about this.*

Except Ash. The person she'd taken home to get her mind off life, the one she'd wanted to use for orgasms but keep at a safe distance, had been the one she'd effortlessly opened up to. The one who'd held her when she freaked out with not an ounce of judgment in his eyes.

"I didn't get his number or even his last name. I don't know where he lives—he could just be passing through. He knows where I live, though, so if he wants to see me, it's up to him to come to me."

Delia nodded, looking troubled, then popped another piece of croissant into her mouth. Her expression instantly dissolved into near-ecstasy. "See, all I have to give me that womanly glow is a gigantic box of carbs."

Maddie laughed, exhaling in relief as the pressure of this conversation lifted off her. "I think I'll stick with that," she said, but in truth, if Ash showed up at her door tonight, she knew she'd let him in. And the next night. And the night after that.

Damn. She was so screwed.

"I need a status update from you."

Ash shrugged, not bothering to look at his superior. Metos lounged on his big fucking throne-like chair, stacks of ancient books and scrolls heaped around him.

"No deadlines approaching. All's well," Ash said.

"Is it?"

He fell silent and waited for the castigation to come, whatever it was...though he had a feeling he knew. He'd been falling down on the job lately; he could admit it.

"I notice you have far fewer cases than any of the others. Care to explain why you've grown so lazy?"

"Would it help if I did?"

Metos just stared at him. Ash sighed and continued. "I highly doubt pleading my own case will exonerate me. It never has before."

"What's the matter, Ash? Burned out?"

"Maybe."

"Really. It wouldn't be a matter of your attentions being elsewhere? Like...where they were last night?"

Damn. Caught. Ash cast a glance at the silvery, mirrorlike pool in the corner of Metos's cavernous lair. If one stared into it, one could see the locations of any of the demons loose upon the earth. And exactly what manner of mischief they were up to. He'd mistakenly hoped he wasn't under close surveillance, as one of the oldest and most trusted in his profession. Looked as if that trust had been wearing thin.

"Is there a problem?" he asked carefully. Much as he hated to admit it, it was best to tread with caution lest he end up upside down over a fire pit. Or chained up in a torture dungeon.

Metos reached down over the arm of his chair and picked

up one of the topmost tomes. He opened it and flipped to a page where a black ribbon lay to mark the place. As he did so, a torn piece of parchment flew from the book and landed at Ash's feet, going unnoticed by Metos. Ash leaned over and picked it up, finding words scrawled across it in his master's atrocious penmanship.

Thou shalt purge the abomination, banish the afflicted, for it is an offense Hell cannot deign to hold.

Ash stared at the unfamiliar law. What the fuck was such an offense Hell wouldn't even hold it? He'd never heard of that before. Whatever it was, it must be an extremely rare occurrence. Curiosity getting the better of him, he opened his mouth to ask, but Metos cut him off.

"I'll take that." Ash looked up to find Metos's waiting hand stretched toward him, his eyes narrowed in warning. With a shrug, he handed it back. Must be ultra-top-secret master demon business.

Metos settled back in his chair. "Now. According to my records, your contract with one Maxwell Gatlin for the soul of Madeleine Dean is open-ended. You can move at any time now, but it's been two years. Why haven't you collected?"

"Because it's open-ended," Ash said slowly, as if he were speaking to an uncomprehending child. So much for treading cautiously. "I'm enjoying the game. Choosing my moment to strike."

"And you didn't get it last night?"

"What does it matter? She's ours regardless if I take her now or if I let her live out her entire life and take her at the end of it."

It was the exact same thing he'd been telling himself since she'd lifted his fingers from her chest, from over her beating heart, and kissed the tips. He didn't have to do it now. There would be many, many more opportunities.

"I'm telling you to do it now."

Shit.

Metos went on. "We can't afford these delays. Every day we wait is a day those winged imbeciles can find a way to thwart us. It concerns me that I have to remind you of this. You were once one of my swiftest collectors—why linger now? Take her."

Ash cast his gaze to the floor, refusing to give up anything through his expression alone. He *had* been prepared to strike. Last night. Last night before Madeleine had turned her blue eyes on his. He'd prepared himself again, only to be defeated by the press of her sweet lips against the hand that would've drawn the soul out of her.

"Ashemnon." Ash looked up into the harsh yellow eyes of his master. "I trust you will not allow a minor thing like your lust for this *human* to deter you from claiming what is ours."

"Of course not."

"Excellent. Now get back to the surface and do your job. You don't want me to have to send someone else." The last words seethed with such warning Ash didn't doubt the threat for a moment.

What was he waiting for? He'd had his taste. It was all he'd wanted, just a few hours pressed against and buried inside the exquisite softness of her body. Metos was right, and Ash had said as much to the angel up on the surface. To delay was to invite peril. He didn't think he'd left any loopholes—the whole thing was simplicity itself—but as he'd learned the hard way a couple of times, one could never be too cautious. And he couldn't afford to care about anything other than staking his claim.

Chapter Eight

Maddie didn't mind working at Delia's store at all. That wasn't work. It was getting paid to hang out with friends all day, talking about music. Laughing. It never failed to take her mind off whatever was troubling her.

Her waitressing job was another story.

She tried not to whine too much; at least she had a second job. The place was upscale and the tips were awesome. Besides that, she could always look for another gig somewhere else, if it came to that. But while things mostly sucked there, big time, she hadn't been pushed past that breaking point yet. She was toughing it out.

Still, the situation always seemed far, far worse than usual when she was called in on her night off. Even more devastating was the fact she'd first met David here. He'd come in on a business lunch. She'd spilled a glass of water on his shirt. Ironic, wasn't it, that the very bumbling nature he would eventually leave her over had been endearing to him in the beginning. It had gotten his attention, anyway. He'd dawdled at the table until the rest of his party moved toward the door, and gently caught her wrist as she walked by, slipping his card into her palm. God, she hadn't been able to wipe the goofy grin off her face the rest of the day.

Of course, he'd made her come to him. Bastard.

She could've declined to come in to work, but she'd be crazy to turn down the money. Plus the idea of sitting at home by herself didn't appeal. She would think too much, and that was never a good thing. Maybe leaving would mean missing a knock at her door, but how pathetic would she be to sit around waiting for it? She knew, deep down, it was never going to come.

Was it so wrong to hope, though? She didn't want to sleep alone tonight.

But at the moment, here she was, wearing her pressed white shirt and black slacks with the little black apron tied around front. Carrying her little pad around. Serving all the happy, well-dressed couples on their Saturday night dates. And if in her mind she could picture herself dumping red wine into their designer laps, well, it was her little secret.

For being so frantic to get in touch with her in the middle of the night, David hadn't tried to call or text her once today. Maddie gnawed her lip and tried to concentrate on writing down the convoluted order she was taking, but her thoughts were in turmoil. Did he know what she'd done? Why should she freaking care?

It wasn't as if there'd be any chance of reconciliation. When David made up his mind about something, he was a rock, unmovable. So she hadn't sabotaged anything by her little indiscretion—at least she didn't think so, no matter how many times he'd called last night. There was nothing to sabotage. It was done.

She headed to the back, through the swinging doors, edging around one of the waiters bearing a heavy tray on one shoulder. Her dickhead manager was shouting as usual, his voice like grating glass in her head. She barely registered the words—something about accuracy—as she refilled her water pitcher to make her rounds. Her feet hurt already. Her head hurt. The pleasant afterglow of great sex had long since faded, and she didn't even have the lingering aches to remind her last night had really happened.

She didn't know which loss hurt her more—David or Ash. What did that even say about her? How fucked up was she?

Ugh. She needed a minute alone. Glancing at the clock, she shouted "Break!" and made a beeline for the bathroom. The place was closing in on her right now, and the small bathroom didn't help matters, but at least she was away from the noise and bustling bodies.

Cool water on her face. It felt good, but it couldn't wash away the dirt on her soul.

And wasn't she just a barrel of laughs tonight? Chuckling to herself, she turned the faucet off and glanced up at the mirror—and gasped, slamming her back to the wall of the nearest stall.

Nothing there. Nothing there, but there'd been a face behind her in the mirror, gray and ghastly, mouth open in a soundless howl, a withered hand reaching for her shoulder like the ones in the nightmares.

Oh God, it had never happened *here*, it had never happened outside her home. Oh *God...*

Pull yourself together! Her mind screamed it, but she didn't want to obey because she couldn't deal with this, she really couldn't. The panic attack hit hard, and she slid down to the floor, gasping for breath, heart galloping, not caring, not giving a damn anymore because she was about to absolutely lose her fucking mind, but at least then the pain and the fear might go away...

The door swung open and feet shuffled in. If she'd given a damn about anything she'd have leaped to her own feet and maintained what little composure she could muster. But she didn't. Dana, one of the other waitresses she didn't know that well, came around the corner and stopped dead when she saw her.

"You okay, hon?" Dana asked cautiously.

Maddie nodded, aware of how she must look. Still not caring. Her face was tingling and numb. She had to force her lips into motion, wrench the words from her closed-up throat. "Just give me a minute."

"You sure? Do I need to call—"

"I said give me a fucking minute. *Please.*"

Without another word, Dana stomped from the room. Maddie clambered to her feet, ignoring her violent trembling and trying to keep her heart from tearing its way out of her chest. She splashed more water on her face, getting more on her shirt than her flushed skin. As soon as her palms covered her face, she broke into sobs.

The part of her brain that was still rational tried to soothe her, assured her she was fine, she was still here, she wasn't going anywhere. But the growing black pit of dread and doom that had been spreading inside her for as long as she could remember was poised to swallow her whole now. One day soon, those things were going to get her. Those shrunken, skeletal hands were going to grab her and not let her go. When that happened, it would all be over. Maybe by then she would even go willingly.

Something had a hold on her. Something evil.

Five minutes later, she left the bathroom, having fixed her hair, dried off and composed herself as well as she could. A faint tremor still shook her hands and weakness lapped at her legs, but maybe she could make it through the rest of the night. Suddenly she didn't mind being around people, no matter who

85

they were. She found Dana and mumbled a thanks and an apology, to which Dana shrugged and said, "Fine, whatever."

Her manager rampaged through the kitchen again, so Maddie grabbed her water pitcher and hit the doors lest she become the new object of his incessant ire. She paused to let Lucy, the hostess, walk by in front of her. "Just sat you a couple," the too-perky blonde informed her.

"Thanks." Hopefully after these, the night would start to wind down. She could really use a glass of wine.

Even more so after she glanced over and saw who it was Lucy had seated in her section. And froze in her tracks, causing the waiter behind her with a precariously balanced tray to crash into her.

"Jesus, Maddie! Watch out," he said, but she barely heard him. He managed to hang on to the tray somehow, but her full water pitcher was jostled by their impact. She didn't know how it happened, but ice water sloshed right down the back of the perfectly coiffed hair of the woman sitting just in front of Maddie's right elbow.

The woman screeched. Heads turned, even the sandy-blond one that was the object of Maddie's scrutiny. And the red one sitting across the table from him.

On the other side of the restaurant, beneath the big bay windows, sat David. And he wasn't alone.

What the hell is he thinking?

The idiot knew she worked here! What kind of asshole brought his...his date to the workplace of the woman he'd dumped just the night before?

In his defense—if such a word could even apply in this

case—he'd looked as shocked and mortified as she felt. Well, he did know her schedule pretty well, so he'd most likely thought she wasn't working tonight. But still. Those things changed all the time. He *knew* that.

She sat in her manager's office, taking an ass-chewing for her clumsiness. Wow, it was David all over again as she listened to the tirade. *Get your shit together, Madeleine. Quit fucking everything up, Madeleine.*

You're going to end up just like your mother, Madeleine.

A chill lanced through her, jerking her spine straight. Her boss hadn't actually said that. David had never said that. Her mind supplied it all on its own.

It couldn't be true, could it? Had her mother seen these things too? Something had driven the woman to drugs. Hell, if someone had waved a syringe full of blissful emptiness in front of Madeleine's nose right then, she might have shot it up without a second thought. It was enough to raise the hairs on the back of her neck.

I will never *do that. I will* die *first.* She chanted it over and over in her head, but the idea wouldn't leave her mind.

Her boss sent her home for the night. Apparently Dana had informed him of the state she'd found Maddie in earlier. They probably thought she was having a nervous breakdown. They wouldn't be far off the mark.

Thankfully she didn't have to see David, since she went out the back. The image of the redhead he was with was burned into her memory, though. Maddie could tell she was tall, even folded into her seat. Probably leggy, too, considering the long, sleek length of her toned arms. Her glittery tank dress had been almost the same shade as that magnificent hair. So had her lips. They had been curled with amused pity for the poor clumsy waitress who doused an old lady with ice water.

If she'd known Ash's number, she'd have him on speed dial by now. She needed him to lick her wounds again tonight. And lick her in other places. Until she screamed, until she forgot.

She had almost made it to her Jeep when rapid footsteps began beating a path toward her. As she opened her door, she glanced over to see David almost upon her, his stride brisk.

She tried to jump in her car, but he grabbed her arm with one hand and the door with the other, keeping her from fleeing. "Maddie, please, listen to me. Just two minutes and I'll let you go."

"Fuck you."

"Don't be like that."

"To hell with you, then. Isn't that what you said to me last night? And exactly how am I supposed to *be*? Oh, it all comes clear now. You're an asshole. Let me go before I start screaming."

"It's not what it looks like, I promise—"

Her blood rushed in her ears. "Hmm, let's see. You don't have a sister, or any hot female friends or relatives that I'm aware of. This is someone I'm *not* aware of, and someone I seriously doubt you just met today, so... I'm just doing the math, here."

He blew out a breath and ran a hand through his hair, watching the distant traffic on the freeway for a moment. She locked her gaze on her shoes. "And you brought her *here*," she finished quietly.

"I thought you were off tonight. And this is where she wanted to go." She sensed him flinch at the admission without actually seeing it.

Her instinct was to launch at him with her fingernails, but she might actually do him physical damage. So she stood rigid as a statue, afraid if she so much as twitched a muscle it would undo all of her hard-won control. "How long, David? And who is she?"

Now she was only torturing herself, but she had to know. Had to.

"She works in my building. I've known her two months. But I swear I never cheated on you, Maddie. Tonight is the first time we've ever been out together."

"Bullshit."

"What reason do I have to lie to you at this point? What would I gain? If I'd been fucking her, I'd tell you. But it really doesn't matter if you believe me or not, does it?"

"So you weren't fucking her, but you wanted to. Well, I feel much better about this whole thing."

"If you can't be adult about this—"

"And you are? You don't know how bad I want to slap your face right now. I thought you were better than this, I really did."

His eyes narrowed, twin pools of darkness barely catching the dim light from the overhead lamps. "You didn't seem too broken up about the whole thing last night. At least not enough to stop you from spreading your legs to some fucking stranger. Yeah, I watched you leave with him. I even followed because I couldn't believe what I was seeing. Thought maybe you were just giving him a ride for some reason, thought surely you wouldn't do something like that. I tried to call you because I was worried about you—you don't even *know* that guy." His mouth twisted bitterly. "I guess your mouth was too occupied to talk."

She wanted to retort to that, but choked on the words. He wasn't choking on his; he aimed them at her like darts, and her heart was the bull's-eye. "So don't stand there all insulted because I decided to move on, baby. You've got me beat by a mile."

"That's great, judge me when I'm sure you couldn't wait to get into her pants while we were still together. That is, if you're telling the truth, which I doubt."

"At least I ended things with you first."

"Yeah, you're a real gentleman. Get out of my sight, David. And if you wouldn't mind, stay the hell out of my restaurant."

A smirk marred his features. She'd once thought he was damn good-looking, and yeah, she guessed he was. But now the very qualities that had drawn her to him turned her stomach. Nothing about his face was *interesting*. Cookie-cutter handsome. Like a thousand other guys. Now Ash, on the other hand...

"Well, after that episode tonight, it might not be *yours* for very long," David said.

It took a moment for the words to register because she was actually caught up in a mini-fantasy about the tiny, almost imperceptible dent in Ash's chin. Once they did, she couldn't bring herself to do much more than frown at her ex. Now he was being deliberately hurtful for no good reason.

Wow, how things could change over the course of a day. If not for Ash, and the way he'd made her feel last night, she would probably be a sobbing mess hanging on to David's leg right now, begging him not to leave her. But she'd never been more serious in her life when she looked him in the eye and said, "You're obviously proud of what you've accomplished with this whole situation, so run along and revel in it. And give my regards to what's-her-face in there. She probably did me a favor."

"You're kidding yourself if you think she's the only reason we're here right now. You're a mess, Madeleine. A fucking mess."

She was opening her mouth to reply when a new voice spoke up, one that sent shivers up her spine and set her pulse throbbing between her legs. "I believe I heard the lady ask you to leave her alone."

Ash emerged from around the other side of the car adjacent to Maddie's Jeep. She'd have run from the look on his face if it had been aimed at her. Since it was directed at her ex, the urge to end up a grateful heap at his feet was almost too much to resist. What was he doing here?

David didn't look nearly as happy to see him. He drew himself up to his full six feet—Ash was taller, she noticed with no small amount of glee—and squared his shoulders. *God, please don't let them start brawling here.* "This is a private conversation, if you don't mind." His voice lacked the confidence to make the words much of a menace.

"I mind. The conversation is over."

That voice, on the other hand...

Maddie watched David's reaction, anticipating the worst possible outcome from this scenario. He didn't respond well to threats and he hated to be the first to back down. Judging from the malice rising off Ash in waves, she suspected the same of him. Even though his expression remained calm, almost dispassionate, it was the frightening nonchalance of one who didn't doubt his strength or abilities for a moment. She needed to step in *now*, or this could get ugly fast.

"He's right. I'm done speaking with you, David. I can't imagine there's anything else that needs to be said. Right? It's through, we're over, and keep in mind that was your choice. So just...leave me alone."

He finally tore his intense gaze from Ash's face and fastened it on her, but thankfully the rigid line of his jaw relaxed a bit as he looked at her. "Yeah. Right. Fine." With one

91

final searing look at Ash, he turned and strode toward the restaurant. She watched his retreating back for a moment, feeling numbness settle in the pit of her stomach. That was good. Numb was good. Her old trusty defense mechanism coming to her rescue yet again, just as it had so many times throughout her life. She only wished she didn't need it so damn often.

"Another embarrassing moment you've witnessed," she commented, feeling Ash move to her side. She tipped her head back slightly to look at him. "What are you doing here?"

His delectable lips quirked at one end. "Obviously, I've been following you." She cocked an eyebrow at him, and the tilt of his mouth turned into a full smile. "Kidding. Just happened to be leaving from over there and saw you." He indicated the bar next door, its parking lot separated from the restaurant's by only a curb with a strip of greenery. "Does seem pretty weird, huh?"

"More than a little. *You* weren't with a date, were you?"

"After you? No one would compare."

Maddie rolled her eyes, but a piece of her turned cartwheels from the sweetness of it. "Oh, that was good."

"It was, wasn't it? Good enough to..." He frowned, staring at something over her left shoulder. She looked behind her, but couldn't see anything except the usual scene: the bar, the parking lot, the freeway.

"What is it?"

His face had undergone a transformation, from good humor to a glower she couldn't even begin to interpret. She waved a hand in front of his face, and finally he snapped out of it and looked down at her. "What?" he asked.

"What, what? What do you see?"

"Nothing. So where are you going now?"

"Home." *Do you want to come?* She didn't want to ask that question, not at all. She didn't need to get in any deeper with this guy, because the day of weirdness she'd spent unable to exorcise him from her every thought had unnerved her. Her intense reaction to his mere presence now scared the hell out of her. Already, she was wet, clenching her thighs together against the emptiness burning at their apex. Her breasts felt heavy and needy beneath her bra, her nipples chafing against the simple cotton.

She should be mourning a lost relationship, but she hadn't given it much thought at all until she'd walked into the restaurant tonight. She should still be upset, numb—and maybe she was—but she wanted to drag Ash into her Jeep and fuck him raw right here.

God, he was so good. It was knowledge of that goodness that kept her from stopping him when he suddenly slammed her back against her car with a kiss that scrambled the last of her coherent thoughts into mush. "Shit," she gasped against his lips, and he chuckled. His mouth burned against hers. She'd forgotten about the freaking *heat* he generated. Instantly, her skin warmed everywhere he touched her, and she thought she might be sweating from mere contact with him in no time. When they got back to her place—and there seemed to be no question now that was where they were headed—she was going to stick a thermometer in his mouth.

The thought forced a wild giggle from her throat. His hand tugged her shirt from her pants and, before she could gather her wits enough to warn him people were going to *see*, her breast filled his palm. Which was the only place it really wanted to be. She giggled again.

"What's *with* you?" he asked, laughter in his own voice.

"You just...make me happy. At a time when I really need it."

He paused, then slowly released her. *Hell.* She shouldn't have said that. "I mean, for...oh, damn. Please don't take that the wrong way, I know this isn't—"

Ash lifted a finger to her lips. "Shh. It's all right." His eyes were like twin chips of the night sky, but with no stars. She fell silent, but couldn't resist giving his fingertip a nibble. "It's all right," he repeated. "It's just the first time anyone has ever said something like that to me."

What was wrong with the women he'd known? And what could she say? Granted, she'd known him only for a day. But everything she'd seen so far intrigued her. Even the thought of the intricate tattoos swirling across his back set a slow burn through her veins now. She liked imagining how they'd move over his flexing muscles as she dug her fingernails into his flesh...

"Are we going to stand here all night, or are we going to go do something about *this*?" she asked throatily, slipping her fingers through his belt loops and grinding her hips into him so she could feel his erection against her stomach.

His hands traveled up to her face, capturing her cheeks. She sucked in a breath as he stared into her eyes, her legs melting from under her. "Now there's an invitation I can't resist," he said.

Her lips turned down, bitterness still too close to the surface. "Even though I'm such a fucking mess?"

"But such a pretty mess. I do have to take care of something first, though. Why don't you head to your place, and I'll meet you there in thirty minutes or so."

"Oh. Okay. Are you sure? If it's bad timing—"

"It is, actually. Dreadful timing." He smiled. "But I'm still going to be with you. What does that tell you?"

It told her...this was in serious danger of going exactly

where she hadn't wanted it to go—straight to the heart. But God help her, she wasn't about to stop it.

Chapter Nine

Once he'd tucked Madeleine into her car, given her one more lingering kiss and shut her door, he waited until the Jeep's taillights were out of sight before turning to face the angel who'd so rudely intruded. The same one who'd caught him on the street last night.

"Well?" Ash demanded.

"You have an appointment."

"You've got that right."

"With the mediator."

Fuck! How had the bastard wrangled that? This thing was so cut-and-dried, it couldn't be any simpler. "Why are you even bothering?"

"You know, I asked myself that question, given the circumstances. But I figured better safe than sorry."

"I'm moving on her tonight."

"No, you're not." The angel reached into his robes and pulled out a scroll, which he tossed at Ash's feet. "You've been stayed pending our meeting with Nicolae. Until then, you are barred from claiming her." As Ash glared in speechless outrage at his plans being thwarted before his very eyes, one corner of the angel's mouth hiked up. "Again, not that I really think I needed it. But you *are* hanging around quite a bit, so I figured your superiors would eventually start to get antsy, and you're all so...unpredictable. I'm just covering my bases, you understand."

"You are one cryptic bastard. What's that supposed to mean?"

"You are one delusional demon if you can't figure it out." He turned to go. "We'll be seeing you two weeks from tonight— Nicolae has other engagements for a while. Be there or be prepared to forfeit."

"Other engagements," Ash grumbled. "Hopefully death is one of them." He watched as the winged figure arrowed toward the heavens, swift as a shooting star.

The scroll lay at his feet. He picked it up and unfurled it, giving it only a cursory glance. All looked in order—he really couldn't move on Madeleine pending the outcome of the meeting.

Damn angel was talking crazy, though. He'd often thought they were whacked out of their heads anyway, thinking there could be any good left in this world worth fighting for. This one seemed especially mad.

The mediator. Shit. It wasn't that Ash was concerned, really...but sitting in that study with his careful work under scrutiny was a place no demon wanted to be. It was rare, but there was always the chance for disaster if Nicolae saw something in the contract that made his gray mustache twitch.

But...this gave him a reprieve, too, at least for a short while. He didn't have to worry about taking Madeleine right now.

Wait, what? Since when was he *worried*?

The sudden absence of a weight in his chest proved to him he had indeed been worried about it. Even more troubling, the thought of spending tonight with her, unhindered by the duty

97

that must be done, was...thrilling. No cares. Just him and Madeleine.

Such a simple concept, but the enormity of it rocked him to the core. How would it feel not to have that damn contract looming over every moment he spent with her? He felt almost peaceful.

Snap out of it, idiot. The contract was the reason she *would* be with him, for eternity. Not an eternity she would enjoy, but one in which he could do with her soul as he pleased. She wouldn't be here, walking this earth beyond his reach, tormenting him any longer. The moment he claimed her would be the moment he'd find true peace. He should be angrier, far angrier, about what had just been done to him. But, try as he might, he couldn't muster more than mild annoyance at the angel for being one step ahead.

How could he, when he knew Madeleine was probably arriving at her little apartment at this very moment, thinking of him, waiting for him, anticipating the night ahead? Everything else faded into the far distance. He didn't understand it, but neither was he fighting it.

The promise of one night of peace for his kind, with no scheming or agendas—just pleasure—was far too precious to question.

It was all he could do to kill time, to allow enough of a delay in his arrival that she'd believe he'd run his imaginary errand. His shields were still raised from his conversation with the angel, so prying eyes were no concern. He paced the parking lot, he watched the people coming and going from the restaurant. Couples arm-in-arm. Laughing and snuggling, driving off into the night.

For the first time in his entire existence—far longer than even his earliest memories allowed him to contemplate—he knew exactly how they felt.

Her door flew open after he'd barely tapped on it, and she stood there looking up at him with an eager wide-eyed expectancy he found fucking adorable. "Okay," she said before he could make a move. "You can totally say no if you want. Totally. But my friend called, and when I told her I was off early and, um, seeing you...she asked if we wanted to meet her for a few drinks at this club downtown we like to go to. I just thought, maybe it would be fun to hang out, dance...if you like that sort of thing. If not, that's cool too. I said I'd ask. That's all."

He couldn't stop grinning at her nervous excitement, at her babbling, at the way she practically bounced from one foot to the other. He so did not dance. But if it meant that much to her, hell, he could pretend. "Sure. We can do that."

"Awesome! But will you tell me one thing first?"

"Anything."

"Um...what the hell is your last name? I'm sorry, it's just...I'd like to know."

"All you had to do was ask." He thought fast. "It's Emmons."

"Emmons. Ash Emmons. Great. And I'm Madeleine Dean, in case, you know, in case you were wondering."

He clasped her hand in his and brought it to his lips. "Charmed, Madeleine Dean." Oh, was he ever. She beamed at him, her blue eyes bright, her white teeth sinking into her plump lower lip.

"So, um...will you tell me some more about you?"

Great. She tugged him into her apartment and closed the

door behind him, shutting out the rush of traffic and a gaggle of voices from the parking lot. "What do you want to know?"

"Like...do you live here?"

"No. I don't."

"Oh." He saw her face fall even though she obviously tried to maintain an air of cheerfulness. "Where are you from?"

"Here and there. I move a lot." Dammit, he had to do better than that. But she was already moving toward her bedroom, having accepted his nonanswer with good grace.

"Must be interesting. I'm going to take just a few minutes and change, okay?"

"All right." Now he felt like an ass...and, in the grand scheme of things, that was ridiculous. "I live in Houston right now." He'd been there on enough assignments to know it was a nice comparison to his true place of origin. He quite liked it.

"Wow!" she called from her room. "I never would've thought. You don't sound like— But then, I guess you wouldn't, since you move a lot. Duh. Are you here on business or pleasure?"

Business that has very unexpectedly turned into pleasure.

"Business."

"The contract stuff you don't like to talk about, huh? Sorry."

He reserved comment and ambled over to the parrot's cage, which she had rolled into the living room at some point. The bird was perched inside, utterly still and gazing impassively at him. His feathers were jewel green, except for an explosion of yellow around the face. "Demon," he chirped.

"You know it," Ash muttered. The almost intelligent, *assessing* way the bird stared at him was disturbing.

Madeleine emerged from her bedroom a minute later, wearing a slinky black top and jeans that hugged her curves in

100

all the right places. Her hair was a wild, glorious cascade of curls. His mouth began to water. The bird wolf-whistled accordingly. She laughed and spied Ash standing near the cage. "Making friends?"

If he'd quit calling me out, sure, we'd be great friends. Yeah, the parrot's name was supposed to be Demon, but...looking into those beady little bird eyes, he couldn't help but wonder. Animals didn't like his kind as a rule, but thankfully, most animals couldn't talk.

"Hey," Madeleine said, approaching him and reaching up to fiddle with the zipper of his leather jacket. "I'm sorry."

"For what?"

"Well, I knew what was up when I brought you here last night, and now I'm pressing for your life history like this is something that... I'll stop, okay? You just tell me what you want, when you want. *If* you want."

He stared down at her, her angelic beauty, the cerulean blue gaze that somehow managed to be shy even as it was direct. She would be—*should* be—any mortal man's dream. Yet again he thought of that poor clueless bastard who'd let her go last night. And hurt her tonight. A slow burn of fury slithered through his blood. "The truth is, Madeleine..." She stared expectantly at him, her breath held. "I'm only in town for a couple of weeks."

"Okay," she said, nodding vigorously. "I get it."

"No, it's...complicated." He reached up to push a curl from her forehead, allowed his fingertips to linger on the soft, unlined flesh. So vibrant. Now he could feel her roiling emotions. Something had happened to her tonight, and the fear hadn't left her yet. "But if it's all right with you," he continued, "I certainly wouldn't mind your company while I'm here."

"It's all right with me," she said, but he thought her voice was tinged with the hint of sadness he could feel emanating from her. Or maybe that was only because he was listening for it. "I appreciate your directness. So we'll just...have fun while you're here, then?"

"Sounds like a plan."

She smiled. Something broke in his chest. For the first time in his existence, Ash actually entertained the thought of thanking Nicolae. After she smiled at him with such sweetness, such *trust*, there was no way in Hell he could have taken her tonight, and he would have been in a world of shit as a result.

He might be already. Because he'd begun to wonder if there was any way he could take her at all.

"Well, he can't dance," Delia proclaimed a couple hours later, shouting to be heard over the music. "But he's hot enough to make up for it."

Madeleine giggled and downed a good portion of her apple martini. Ash had drifted off somewhere, presumably to the men's room, so they had a moment for a brief powwow as they stood at a table a safe distance from the writhing bodies on the dance floor. "Oh, he's not that bad."

"Nah, not that bad. If he's got the moves to give you the look I saw on your face this morning, there might be hope for him yet."

"Not that it matters. For me, anyway. He told me tonight he's leaving in two weeks."

Delia turned smoky eyes on her. "So?"

"So...so it was said in a way that was sort of...putting me in my place. I mean—no, that sounds harsh. He wasn't rude at all. But he made it pretty clear this was just a fling, and I'm okay with that."

The smoky eyes narrowed. "No, you're not."

"Well...it's better than nothing for the next two weeks."

"So's a vibrator. Sometimes you need a big dick without having to deal with the bigger dick attached to it."

"Don't do that. If I wasn't in agreement with this situation, all I'd have to do is say so. I just want to have some fun. It's kind of...freeing, in a way, not to have to worry about trying to land him. He's going to be gone anyway."

"Bullshit, Mad. We don't live in the days of horse-drawn buggies or whatever. We live in the age of online dating and relationships that span fucking continents. Hop a plane and you can be with him in a couple of hours. You keep it going with this guy, and you'll end up falling hard, daydreaming about weekend getaways to see him and stuff like that. Then he'll be gone back to his life and you'll *still* be brokenhearted."

Maddie twirled her drink on its thin coaster, feeling the downward pull of the corners of her mouth. She didn't actually hear Delia sigh, but got the general impression she did. Her friend turned up her beer and watched the crowd for a moment, looking thoughtful. Then she reached over and put a hand on Maddie's wrist.

"All right, look. I don't mean to rain on your parade."

Maddie shook her head. "No, if you weren't exactly right, then I wouldn't be upset."

"I don't want to be right," Delia said. "And yes, I was cheering for the guy this morning, but I don't like him making an arrangement with you where he gets his jollies for a couple of weeks and you're left picking up the pieces again after he's gone. I want you to get whatever you want out of this deal. But I see the little wheels spinning already, and I'm afraid what you'll end up wanting is white picket fences. And there's nothing wrong with that. It's just that you keep looking for them in the slums."

"David wasn't necessarily the—"

"David was the *crown emperor* of the slums."

Maddie laughed. "So what you're saying is you think I have zero chance of making Ash fall madly in love with me in two weeks?" She allowed a sly little grin as she asked it.

Delia pointed two fingers at her. "A-*ha*. Caught ya." Maddie shoved her playfully, and her friend went on. "He'd be a fool not to, sweetie. I know that, and *you* know that…"

"Right. Here he comes."

Madeleine wished the smile she plastered on her face as he rejoined them wasn't so fake. She'd been in such a fabulous mood earlier, thinking of spending the night with him, but the whole thing about him being here temporarily had put a damper on her elation. She wished she could forget it and live for the moment, which had been her spectacular plan last night when she'd met him. And now she'd gone and let herself get caught up again, over the course of only *one day*. How bad would it be if she saw him over the next two weeks?

Maybe she really was grieving for David and was sort of projecting all of that anguish onto Ash somehow. Because he was here to project it onto. Maybe that was the kind of fucked-up psychological thing that happened when you got bounced from one guy's bed, only to bounce another guy into yours with no downtime in between.

See, if you had a therapist you could ask her these things.

Delia kept up a stream of chatter and witticisms with Ash despite the unsavory nature of her and Maddie's prior conversation about him. Bless her. But the flashing lights and pulsing music were beginning to wear on Maddie's nerves, and before long she and Ash were saying good night. Delia hugged her and slinked her way back onto the dance floor.

Outside, the air was cool and fresh, and Maddie breathed it deep to clear out all the mingling scents of cologne, perfume and sweat from her nostrils. Because she hadn't been sure about how much they would have to drink, they'd taken a cab to the club. But Ash seemed content to stroll along the sidewalk with her, their fingers interlaced.

"Did you have fun?" she asked finally, when the silence had stretched out for far too long. But again, like last night, she was struck by how it wasn't awkward at all, it just...was.

"This is more fun. You. Me. Relative silence."

"I agree. I did need to get out for a little while, though. My ex didn't care for the club scene—well, he didn't like Delia at all. I never told her that, though."

"He doesn't like much of anything."

She looked over at him. "Huh?"

Ash shrugged. "Just the general impression I got. He's a miserable person overall. He has no idea what he really wants."

Wow. Ash had just very astutely nailed an aspect of David's personality it had taken her months to figure out, and he'd only spoken a handful of words to him. Then again, she often felt the same way about herself: miserable, uncertain. Maybe the same qualities hadn't stood out so much in David because one miserable person could be fairly comfortable with another one. Until they started to drag each other even further down.

"I should've done more with my life," she grumbled. How that thought factored in to their current conversation, she didn't really know—only that it often occurred to her when she was feeling down.

"Like what?"

"I don't know, gone to college or something. I didn't do well in school. Not that I'm dumb or anything. I was lazy. I didn't see much point in it at the time. There was too much chaos in my life on top of everything. I got into some trouble, but I managed to not go down the same path as my mom."

He walked along beside her, gaze downcast. She'd have thought she was boring him, but the slight furrow of his brow made her think he was actually listening intently.

"I know it's never too late," she went on. "But it sure seems like it is. Everything is so...dead end."

"What do you wish you'd done differently? I mean, what would you like to be?"

"I want to help people," she said. "I don't know how, though. It's a moot point anyway—I've never even been able to help myself. I keep myself afloat and that's about all I can manage. But I'd love to...I don't know, be involved with something bigger than myself. I feel like I missed a calling somewhere along the road."

"Hmm," he said, and she laughed.

"I guess you're thinking I don't know what the hell I want, either."

"No, not at all. I was just thinking...it makes sense you'd want to help people."

"Really? Why is that?"

"Seems to be your nature."

"Yet again, I get the uncanny feeling you know me somehow."

He didn't reply beyond a curious little smile that barely tilted up the corners of his mouth.

God, Delia was so right, as much as Maddie wanted to deny it. She wanted to keep telling herself she was a big girl and she could handle it. She *could*, she knew—but this would only inflict undue heartache on her. It was dangerous to keep assigning these romantic notions to anything he said.

Sighing, she cast a quick glance around at their surroundings. The buildings had gradually turned more and more decrepit as they walked, some of them adorned with elaborate graffiti, dotted with dark, cracked windows. She imagined hidden eyes watching from inside them. The street here was eerily empty. "Hey, I didn't notice how far we'd come. We'd better head back. This isn't the best neighborhood."

"As long as you're with me, you don't have to worry about it."

"Cocky, aren't we?"

He chuckled, turning them both and picking up her hand again. "All right. We'll head back."

They hadn't made it twenty feet when her worst nightmare materialized in front of them. Well, one of her worst nightmares, anyway—there were so many. But this one wasn't a ghostly figure; it was a very solid, very real human form that stepped from the alley they were approaching, holding a gun at the end of its outstretched arm.

His face was gaunt, pale, and even from here, she could see he was missing most of his front teeth. Oh, crap. Most likely a junkie, and they were about to provide funds for tonight's fix. Or die. Or both. Her entire body froze up, and she clutched Ash's arm, unable to look away from the gleaming weapon.

"Gimme your wallet, man. And the bitch's purse."

Her heart was about to explode. She didn't think Ash had tensed up at all. "Out of our way," he said, his voice damn near a growl, "before I waste you."

Was he *insane*? "Ash," she hissed. "Just give him what he wants—" She made a move to toss over her clutch, but Ash caught her wrist before she could.

107

"You better listen to your bitch, dude." He brandished his gun. For the first time, Maddie noticed the tremors racking him. "I ain't playin'."

"I ain't either, *dude*. Call her a bitch again and I'll turn you into mine." She watched Ash in utter disbelief. He was entirely focused on their assailant, and something burning in his eyes was...scaring her. It scared the guy too. He took a step back. "That's right," Ash went on. Very slowly, he was distancing himself from Maddie and, though her instinct was to hang on to him, she stayed put. "Back away now. Those shakes are rough, aren't they? You couldn't hit one of us if you tried." He scoffed. "In fact you probably can't even afford bullets."

Oh God, he was only agitating him, and he was doing it on purpose, as if he got some kind of sick thrill out of it.

The gun rose to point straight at Ash's nose. "Keep talkin', man, and I'll show you a bullet up close and personal. I ain't telling you again. Gimme the money."

Ash didn't even flinch. He walked closer. "However much it is, it won't be enough. You know it. You have a beast inside you, and you'll never be able to feed it enough for it to stop eating you alive."

The gun shook violently. If Ash wanted, he could grab it. But he didn't. "What the fuck's wrong with you, man?" the guy asked, his voice wavering on the edge of desperation now.

"Walk away."

"I *need* it—"

"Walk away. Fire that gun, and I'll fuck you up."

Fire that gun and you'll be dead! Madeleine shrieked on the inside. She couldn't even make sense of what she was seeing. Except for one thing. Blind, senseless rage was filling the man's eyes now, and she saw the instant he passed the point of no return, knew instinctively it signaled imminent disaster. It was the same look she'd always seen on her mother before she felt her hand whack her across the face, only ten times deadlier. Her heart stuttered and nearly stopped.

"Fuck you!" The gun went off, the bang and ensuing echo deafening as it bounced off the buildings surrounding them. Madeleine screamed and ducked, her hands over her ears. Despite all his brave words, there was *no way* that shot had missed Ash, oh *God*—

She glanced up to the sound of scuffling feet. Ash wasn't lying on the ground like he should be. He'd grabbed the man and slammed him against the brick wall nearby, holding him with only his palm against the man's chest. The gun was on the ground. The guy was screaming as if he'd taken the shot, but Maddie didn't see any blood. All she saw was Ash's fingers digging hard into his chest. Then the mugger collapsed, falling to the ground in a lifeless heap.

"What did you do?" Maddie cried. Her heart thundered as loud as the gunshot, and her knees would hardly support her weight.

"Nothing. He's unconscious. Let's get out of here."

"Are you hurt?"

He grabbed her hand and propelled her down the sidewalk. She staggered, managed to catch her footing. "Not a scratch," he said.

"But we need to report this, we need to wait for the police—"

"No harm done. We're fine, he's fine."

"He doesn't look fine!"

"He is."

"What did you do to him?"

"A little technique I learned."

"What, the five-point-fucking-palm-exploding-heart technique?"

They cut through an alley to a parallel street, and another and another, weaving around Dumpsters and debris until Maddie's breath wheezed through her lungs. Ash's hand pulling hers was all that was keeping her up, keeping her going. She remained silent as he hailed a cab and shoved her inside first with a hand on her ass.

What had just happened? She couldn't speak, still numb from shock, as Ash gave the driver her address and settled back in his seat. He turned his dark gaze on her and reached up to stroke her hair. Her eyes closed. Tears threatened, and she didn't want them. She wanted to hold it together.

"Okay?" he asked.

She managed a nod, her fingers clenched so tightly around the purse in her lap they ached. He noticed, gently extricated it from her grip, and gave her his hand to hold on to with her death grip.

He wasn't affected by this at all. He wasn't trembling, wasn't even breathing heavy. His gaze on her was steady, assessing. She looked at him, watched the lights from the street pass across his face.

He'd saved her life. Even if the bullet had missed them both, he'd placed himself between her and that gun. He could be dead right now, and that guy needed to be behind bars for it. If their mugger was really okay, why wasn't Ash eager to let the police handle the matter?

But he hadn't *done* anything that she'd seen. The mugger hadn't been bleeding. So how could he be dead by a simple hand against his chest? She saw again in her mind the way he'd fallen, like a puppet whose strings had been cut. No strength in his limbs whatsoever.

Ash pulled closer to her, putting his mouth barely an inch from her ear and murmuring, "Madeleine, it's okay. I promise. You're safe now."

She took a deep breath. The black sparkles that had been filling her vision began to recede somewhat. His touch skimmed over her shoulder, behind her neck, until he was embracing her. Then, with his comforting warmth around her and his hands so gentle on her, she nearly lost it. Her fingers clenched on his shirt, fisting it until she thought she'd rip the fabric.

He kept whispering soothing nonsense and, somehow, incredibly, she began to believe it. She was okay. He was okay. That guy back there, he was probably okay too, but even if he wasn't, he'd tried to freaking kill them. They might not have walked away from that encounter with their lives even if they'd done what he wanted.

Though Ash had seemed to deliberately provoke him, almost as if he'd gotten off on it.

And was she absolutely insane that, despite her fear in the middle of the situation, she'd...*liked* it? Not necessarily to see someone get hurt, but... Oh, hell, she might as well face it. David would have grabbed her purse out of her hand and thrown it at the guy without even the thought of pulling such a badass—if terribly unwise—intimidation tactic.

Who the hell *was* he?

"Thank you," she whispered in his ear. He exhaled as if hearing the words was a relief he'd been waiting for, and his lips grazed her neck. She sighed, threading his soft hair through her fingers. Her panic folded up and disappeared, but the remaining adrenaline from their ordeal was stirring excitement in other far more pleasurable areas. It was shameful to admit, but suddenly all she could think about was ripping his jeans open and—

111

She didn't know what was wrong with her, what he was doing to her. His hand grazed her breast and a quiet explosion went off inside her. Her hips surged toward him, and she could scarcely refrain from climbing over onto his lap. "I want you," she told him, quiet enough that their driver couldn't hear. But Ash's answering growl...he probably *did* hear that. She didn't care. Ash wouldn't have to push very hard and she would probably sprawl back and give it to him right here in the backseat of the taxi.

"I'm going to have you in so many ways tonight," he promised, kissing a path upward to her lips.

"You are so bad for me."

"You are so good for me."

She didn't understand how that was true, but then his mouth covered hers, and it didn't matter. She moaned. Hot, wet, tasting of the drinks he'd had at the club and something deeper, something nameless but profoundly erotic. With every thrust of his tongue into her mouth, the need growing between her thighs doubled.

As bad as he might be, her body didn't care. She needed him in as many ways as he'd promised to have her.

He was still stunned, off balance. She couldn't see it, he made sure of that. The front door to her apartment slammed behind them and he staggered into her bedroom with her clinging to him haphazardly, their mouths fused. The only way to keep her away, to keep her separate, was to get inside her. Keep her as disoriented as he felt, unable to see inside him at what she'd done.

What she'd done...

He'd just saved her life. Again. That wasn't what he was here for. He was here to kill her, inflict physical and spiritual death, and an opportune moment had just presented itself. What she didn't realize was their unwelcome visitor had every intention of ending them right there on the sidewalk, and he'd had to draw his fire or Madeleine could have very well died right there.

He couldn't predict what might happen to her anymore. Everyone had a set time to die, but they also had free will that could cast them into a gray area. Usually that involved entering a contract with one of his kind, like Gatlin. Or pissing one of them off, which was the reason the mugger was a soulless heap on the concrete right now. Madeleine was a question mark as well, now that Ash was an influence in her life.

If she'd died tonight, he wouldn't have been able to take her because of the stay, but the hard part would've been over. Her spirit would roam free, lost and mystified, just like that bastard who'd dared threaten her was doing now. Ash would go back and deal with that one later.

He was as shaken from that encounter as she, but for an entirely different reason. Never once had it even occurred to him to let her die. He'd have torn the man limb from limb if she'd had so much as a scratch on her.

Get inside her. Fuck her hard, over and over, get her out of his system. It was the only way. He tore her jeans down. She was trying to help, but he knocked her hands away, too impatient for her interference. Her fingers went straight to her panties, tugging them down too. "Don't rip these!" she insisted, and he acquiesced and allowed her to strip them off her legs.

Then she was open, and ready, so pink and wet. He couldn't spare her the time to prepare her for his entrance; he freed his cock from his jeans, reached over to search through the drawer for one of the hated sheaths that were completely unnecessary but that she would insist upon. Once it was rolled in place, he guided himself to her pussy and shoved.

Her hips wrenched off the bed to take him, but her hands pushed at his shoulders, fingers clenching around his shirt. "Oh God!" she gasped.

She might be tender from all their vigorous activity last night, so he gave her a moment, murmuring nonsense meant to soothe her. He would say anything, tell her anything she needed to hear, if she'd only let him stay right here, wrapped up tight in her wet oblivion. If she'd let him take her the way he needed to, hard, fast, *now*. "Madeleine," he rasped out.

"Do it, fuck me." She undulated her hips, inflicted sensual devastation on him.

Unholy Hell, that was it. "Yes," he growled. She was throwing so many emotions at him right now, he couldn't distinguish one from the other. Sparing her nothing, he unleashed all his frustrations on her, slamming into her as if he could fuck it all away. Her head tipped back, exposing the pale, graceful column of her throat, her writhing emotions dissolving into bliss. All of them. The fear, the pain, the numb shock of her earlier trauma. Wiped away.

This was the only truth between them.

His gaze wandered over her pink, swollen lips, her closed, fluttering eyelids. He shoved a hand under the shirt she still wore and worked until her bare breast was in his palm. Soft, heavy, the nipple hard as a little pebble for him. He remembered sucking them until she came and almost lost himself.

It wasn't enough. It never would be. Angry at his impending loss of control, he wrenched her legs up and over his shoulders, turning his head to bite the inside of her calf hard. The position seemed to give him access to new depths in her pliant body, and he groaned as he sank inside her to the hilt. He needed every inch of her.

"Oh," she gasped. "God, you're..."

"Tell me," he said when her words trailed off into a moan. "I'm not hurting you, am I?"

"No, just like that, please, don't stop, don't..."

His grin couldn't have been anything short of feral. Obviously she had him mistaken for someone else if she thought anything could tear him away from her at that moment. He looked down at where they joined, lost his breath at the sight of her stretched around him. Her internal muscles gripped him, quivered, tightened until he could hardly breathe. She had to come or she was going to kill him.

He stroked his thumb across her slick clit, feeling her jerk in reaction. "Yes!" she cried. "Please, please!"

As much as he needed to see her release, feel it milk him of the rest of his control, he wanted to draw it out. It wasn't to be. A couple more caresses and she was lost, her fingernails digging crescents into his biceps, her hips grinding on him. He nearly folded her in half with his need to push as deep as he could into her, absorb every ripple of her pussy along the entire length of his cock. Her sweet, lilting cries circled in his head, dying away as the last of her contractions faded and she went limp under him.

He gave her no time to recover. Rolling to his back, he pulled her on top of him, still hard and throbbing inside her. She squeaked but didn't protest, instead dropping her forehead to his shoulder. Ash grabbed her ass with both hands, held her steady and open, and continued driving into her.

Madeleine's face turned toward him, nuzzling his neck. She gave it a little bite and pushed her fingers into his hair, her panting breath hot against his skin. He groaned and pulled her up for a kiss, her taste flooding his mouth as their tongues teased and dueled. He would never forget how she tasted as long as he prowled the caverns of Hell.

It was that realization and the ensuing agony as much as the feel of her slick pussy clamped tight around him that drove him over the edge. It was his turn to dig his fingers in, denting the soft globes as he ground her down on him, spilling his seed into the hated barrier between them. He wanted to thrust it so deeply into her that he would be a part of her being forever. That she would belong to him from now to eternity.

He didn't expect her to come again so quickly, but she did, his pleasure a trigger for her own. She cried out into his mouth and rocked against him as he growled his wordless reply.

Fuck, she was exquisite. He hadn't expected this. Hadn't thought it would make a difference one way or the other if he had a taste of her before he struck. But it had made *all* the difference.

She sighed as she came down from whatever heights he'd taken her to. Her body relaxed, gently draping over him. He slid his hands up her sweat-slick back and hugged her close. "After last night I never thought I'd feel this way again. Never thought I'd see you again."

"I couldn't stay away," he whispered.

Another truth between them.

Chapter Ten

It was hard to brush one's teeth with someone else's teeth nibbling at one's neck. Maddie giggled and slapped at Ash, managing to dislodge a bit of toothpaste foam from her mouth. Despite her squealing efforts to catch it, it dribbled down her black nightshirt.

She dabbed at it with her free hand, pulling her toothbrush from her mouth. "Ah! Look what you did."

"How tragic," Ash said, strolling from the room now that the damage was done.

"I'm going to get you for that. Now I'm stained for the night."

"As if you're going to be wearing it for very long," he commented from the bedroom.

She shuddered in anticipation. Nearly a week had passed since the incident on the street, and every night, Ash had come over. Every night, he'd given her the best orgasm of her life. Which meant, frighteningly enough, that it was only getting better.

She didn't know what was happening, but she wasn't complaining. How could she? The sex was absolutely astronomical—she found herself floating up there around Jupiter every time he so much as touched her.

It couldn't be that she'd found the one. Not like this. Not when he still hadn't said one word about what might happen after he went home. This probably wasn't good for her; she constantly swung between moments of elation and uncertainty, but hell, when had that ever been any different?

Those moments of uncertainty really only seemed to plague her when he wasn't here with her, though, and he was now. She wasn't going to ruin what time they had.

Grinning goofily at her reflection, she stuck her hands under the warm water running from the faucet and leaned over to rinse out her mouth—and came up with a scream caught in her throat.

Blood poured from her faucet, red and obscene in the white sink. She yanked her hands back, nearly choking when she saw that it covered them both and dripped from between her fingers to splatter on the countertop. She reeled backward, catching a glimpse in the mirror as she did so of a silently screaming gray face—and her own shriek finally tore free. She threw herself forward again, whirling around and slamming her butt against the counter.

Of course, nothing was behind her. And nothing came from her faucet now except clear water that swirled harmlessly down the drain.

Ash appeared in the door with a frown in place as she stood there trying not to fall down, her eyes wide, her chest heaving.

"Are you okay?" he asked, his gaze raking her from her bare feet to her pale face. She knew it was pale because she always looked like death itself after one of her episodes.

Normally, her answer to that question was "yes" followed by fake composure, or "no" and an absolute breakdown. What came out this time was, "Will I ever get used to it?"

"Get used to what?"

"After all these years...you'd think I'd get *used* to it. But I don't. Every time I see something, it's as bad as the first time."

He stepped inside the room, taking her trembling hands in his. "What did you see?"

She glanced down into the pristine white sink. "It was running with blood. And...the faces. In the mirror. I saw them again. I saw them the other night at the restaurant too. It's never happened outside wherever I lived before, Ash. It's following me now. But what the hell am I talking about—it's always followed me, no matter where I go—"

Her voice grew higher, tinged with hysteria, and Ash closed what little distance was left between them to pull her into his arms, murmuring that it would be all right.

"Am I losing my mind?" she whispered into the hot flesh of his naked shoulder.

"No," he said. He sounded so certain.

"How can you say that? What *is* this, then? Seeing things that aren't there...that's crazy, right? There's no other explanation. That's—"

"Haunted," he said softly.

She pulled away from him at that, looking up into his dark eyes. They stared back, assured, steady...dispassionate, really. As if he dealt with this sort of thing all the time. "Haunted? You mean like a poltergeist?"

"Or worse."

Maddie scoffed. "I've wished it could be something like that, something there was even the slightest chance I could get rid of. But honestly...I don't believe in those things."

"After everything you've seen? How can you not? Because you aren't crazy, Madeleine. You're absolutely coherent."

"That doesn't matter. And it doesn't feel that way."

With both hands, he smoothed the hair back from her face. "It looks that way. I think...you're very strong."

Strong? No, no one would ever say she was strong. What was the matter with him? "That's the last word I'd use to describe me."

"No, that's the last word you think others would use to describe you...others like your ex. But I want you to forget about all of that. Even if you don't believe what I say about you being haunted, believe that you are not weak, and you are not crazy."

"So...just say that you're right, and this...thing, this entity...is following me, how do I get rid of it? It's happened ever since I was a little girl, no matter where I live. It's me it's after, for whatever reason."

"But you're still here," he said, looking down at her with an assessing gaze she didn't understand. He said it almost as if he were puzzled, but it was the exact same thing she told herself over and over when she was trying to calm down. Then he blinked and glanced around. "Are you finished in here? Come on to bed."

She turned off the faucet and allowed him to pull her out of the bathroom, but she couldn't help casting one last apprehensive glance toward the mirror. All she saw was her own face this time, pale, shadowed...haunted.

"The first time I remember it...really remember it...I was fourteen," she said. They were lying face-to-face, fingers interlaced. "Things had happened before that, but they were minor. Infrequent. But on my fourteenth birthday, I saw the gray faces for the first time. My grandparents had a party for me—one of the few times they did anything like that. I spent the

120

whole thing curled up in the corner of my bedroom, crying. They couldn't get me to come out. I guess that's why I never got another party. I think they had the same problem with me that most people do—they were scared shitless of me."

He could almost understand. Sometimes he was scared shitless of her too.

"It was really bad for me in the beginning. I tried to hide what was happening from my family and the few friends I had, and I got pretty good at it, even though I don't think I used a mirror my entire freshman and sophomore years if I could help it. I wore my hair in a ponytail and didn't bother with makeup. Wasn't ever a fashion plate—I just didn't care."

"You seem to now."

Her faraway gaze was directed at him, but he knew she didn't see him. "I finally decided to suck it up. When I was sixteen, this guy I liked started showing some interest, and I was so eager to go out and be normal I tried to pretend none of it was happening, for him and for myself. That didn't last, of course. Guys came and went and I tried to hide it from most of them. David was the first one I really let in, thinking we were close enough and he cared enough that he could handle it. He couldn't. But can I really blame him? It's not his fault."

"Can you blame him for being a coward who deserted you? Yeah, pretty easily."

"I guess so." She sighed. "But it's best to let it go. I got so frustrated being afraid all the time, and I still do. I get almost defiant about it. Thing is, I'll feel that way one day, and the next I'll be a mess."

Defiant. Oh, she could be. He'd known her long enough to know how strong she was, even if she didn't agree. She'd always been beyond his reach, and he'd tried so many times to get to her. It had never worked, until now—and even then he'd had to exploit the weakness of someone else.

He'd come close once long ago—or at least, closer than any of his other attempts in centuries past. She'd been burned at the stake as a witch in some long-forgotten village in England, when all she'd been guilty of was helping ease women through the rigors of childbirth. One wretchedly cold winter's day, she'd been reluctantly called to the bedside of a nobleman's wife who was nearing the end of her strength during a particularly grueling labor, only to lose both the mother and the child despite all her efforts.

Naturally, the idiots blamed her—they'd called her a witch, the devil's handmaid. Surely she consorted with demons to receive her healing powers. Funny how the people had been happy to make use of them until she failed the wrong person.

If only the fools had known a real demon had revealed himself and propositioned her the night before her execution, and she'd reviled him.

He would never forget that night. Even in the cold, dank stench of the cell they'd pitched her into, even knowing what she faced on the morrow, she'd remained steadfast. She'd been down on her knees when he'd come to her, her hands folded and her head tilted back toward the ceiling. Full lips murmuring prayers. Despite the dire circumstances of the moment, he'd thought of having her on her knees for an entirely different reason, putting those lips to a far more productive use.

He should have known it was futile, but desperation had driven him. He was about to lose her *again*, and who knew how long he would have to wait this time to find her when she came back—*if* she came back? He'd been prepared to offer her anything, pay any price just to have her now, but he had to tread carefully.

"Good evening, madam," he'd said, trying to sound

innocuous.

Apparently he wasn't good at it. She'd taken one glance at him and scurried to her feet, backing against the wall. Yes, it had been far harder for his kind to walk among the masses in those days. Far more of a challenge, far more fun to try. Even in the darkness, he could see the searing blue of her wide eyes, the milky smoothness of her skin. The moonlight glowing off the snow-covered landscape outside her window managed to show him every detail of her delicate face.

She'd stood there, gently panting with her untamed curls loose around her dirty cheeks, looking like a woodland nymph he'd startled. She didn't speak, but waited for him to continue. He'd ached so hard to tear his way into that room and possess her, he nearly ground his teeth to dust. He'd looped his fingers around the bars and clenched them hard to keep from doing so. "If there were any way possible to escape your fate," he'd begun, staring hard through those bars into her panicked eyes, "would you take it?"

It was all he was allowed to ask until she answered in a manner consistent with his plans for her, but he'd known it was a lost cause before he finished the question.

Despite her obvious discomfort with him there, her voice had rung out strong and true. "I would not. I would not lie to save myself. Nor would I blaspheme, or sell my soul. I'll face the flames on the morrow and find my peace in eternity before I face the everlasting fires of Hell."

It was done, then, hopeless. He'd known she saw the fury rise in his eyes, no doubt turning them crimson at having lost her yet again. He hadn't been able to resist one final barb. "Shall I ask again, then, when the first of the flames licks the flesh from your body? I should think you'd be much more amenable then."

"Get thee behind me, Satan!" she'd cried.

The words themselves had hurt, all but throwing him backward. He'd snarled at her and whirled away, scarcely able to rein in his savagery as he stalked down the corridor away from her.

And he watched her die in agony the next morning, wanting to scream, wanting to stop it somehow. Not because he wanted to end her pain—there would be plenty of that where he planned to take her. But because she should be *his*. The fire had devoured her mercifully fast and the angels had winged down from Heaven to carry her soul home. One of the bastards had seen him there among the onlookers and smirked at him before they shot off and disappeared into the ice-blue sky.

Who was smirking now?

Actually, not him, not at the moment. It took effort to pull his thoughts away from that crisp, terrible winter morning so long ago, but it was over. And he was here, in Madeleine's bed, where it was warm and dark and he was...wanted. She snuggled against his chest, her breath cool and minty sweet. The memory of her down on her knees in feverish prayer still wreaked havoc on him, though, and while he'd be content to let her drift to sleep—she needed it—he was so hard it hurt.

As if to make the decision for him, she tilted her head up and her lips brushed his. Her fingers slid down to lightly stroke his cock, and every muscle in his abdomen clenched. "Is this for me?" she asked teasingly.

He could only groan her name in reply and sink into her kiss. Plunder the mouth he'd dreamed would someday murmur desperate pleas for deliverance to him rather than to Heaven. Here it was at last; it was his.

"Oh, Ash," she sighed against his lips.

"I love the sound of that," he said. "Love to hear you say my name."

He felt her smile. "Ash."

"Again."

She repeated it on a giggle, over and over. He laughed, nibbling her lush bottom lip—which made it difficult for her to speak, but still she tried. He nipped his way down the line of her jaw to her throat, which she bared for his exploration. "Thank you for listening to all my insanity," she said as he kissed and gently sucked the place where her pulse beat so strongly against her skin. "For understanding me. You don't know how much it means..."

Her voice trailed away, broken, and he lifted his head to look down at her. Tears glimmered in her eyes. She blinked rapidly as if trying to send them back where they belonged.

It was no use. They belonged to a shattered soul that could never be repaired. Bravely, she forced the words out. "You don't know how much it means to be with someone I feel like I can tell anything to. It's so weird, having known you only a week— or maybe that's why. There isn't any pressure. What do you think?"

Shit. Did she really expect him to talk right now, when her hand was doing that? He studied her face, the subtle nuances of this incarnation. She always looked the same, for the most part. Always blue-eyed, always dark-haired. Her nose was a little sharper this time, her cheeks more rounded. Despite any slight differences, he knew her face better than he knew his own. "Madeleine, I think you're incredible. I think...that's why...oh, *fuck*...that's why this dark entity has attached itself to you."

Her movements ceased, and it was the closest he'd ever come to whimpering like a little girl. Where the hell had *that* come from?

"Really?"

"Well...I mean, I would."

She looked at him for a moment, then laughed. He wanted to crawl under the bed. Yeah. Ha, ha. She thanked him now for being here, but oh, how she would hate him and curse him when she learned the truth. *Get thee behind me*, indeed.

It shouldn't matter, but it did. As she slid her mouth down his chest, kissing a trail toward the epicenter of erotic agony she'd evoked in him, he fisted his hand in her hair and dreaded that day with everything within him.

No sense in denying it any longer. After all this time, all these centuries, she was here, she was his...and if he wasn't contractually obligated to take her, he wouldn't.

Chapter Eleven

Another week passed. Another week ensconced in more bliss than a demon should ever know. He didn't get to spend every waking moment with her, because she was so often at work. There were days he didn't see her at all. But that only made the days when he did all the sweeter.

But it was all over with now. He materialized in front of the grand old house Nicolae called home and, for the first time in centuries, he was nervous. He didn't know what the hell was going to happen here tonight and what implications it could have. The only thing he knew was that he had to get his poker face on, as the humans said. If the angel saw one hint of weakness, Ash would never live it down. He did have a reputation to uphold. He did have a job to do, whether he wanted to or not.

Entering the house, he was greeted with the usual scent of fragrant wax and ages-old tomes, a smell that could portend disaster as easily as success. He fucking hated it here.

Nicolae and the angel were already holed up together in the study, a dim, vast room and the source of the musty ancient-book smell.

Time to put on the mask. Ash smoothed his expression into what he knew was nonchalance of the most arrogant variety and strolled in as if he hadn't a care in the world. The two looked over at the sound of his footsteps.

"Nicolae, my old friend. Aren't you nearing retirement age?"

The angel shook his head, but Nicolae ignored the quip as always, giving Ash a minute nod of greeting. "Your attendance and participation are appreciated."

Ash scoffed and threw himself into one of the gilt chairs sitting in front of Nicolae's massive desk. The thing was so old it was damn near petrified. "It's my understanding they were required."

"You could always forfeit," the angel remarked. "Really, I wouldn't mind."

"I'm sure. So, now that the usual pleasantries are out of the way, let's get down to business." He pulled the contract from his jacket and tossed it on the desk before Nicolae could ask to see it, which he inevitably would. The old man picked it up and unfurled it.

"I love that this is nothing but *business* for you," the angel said.

"Well, what is it for you?"

"Far more than that."

"Oh, come on. You can tell me. Are your numbers dwindling? Not letting as many through the pearly gates? Fighting a losing battle? You should've seen the specimen I reaped a couple of weeks ago. Wore sin like a cloak. I'm really doing you a favor, you know. Saving you from having to deal with the dregs of society fighting for entrance into your pristine utopia, so they don't sully it."

"And Madeleine? Is she one of the 'dregs of society'?"

He felt his demeanor crack. The angel's dark eyebrows rose. *Shit.* "Of course she is. What else would she be?" His voice was too tight for his own liking. He rubbed a hand across his chest, addressing the ache that formed there at speaking about her in such a manner.

"I know one thing she is. She's falling in love with a demon, a creature of such vile filth I shudder to think of it."

"Why are you so distressed? It's just one girl. One soul."

"Because she's a *Candidate*, you swine." The righteous indignation coming off the angel was palpable enough that Ash tilted his head back. The world could have ended in that simple statement.

Madeleine, a Candidate? A special soul in training to gain her wings. He'd known they sometimes chose from the old souls to fill their ranks, but not always. In fact, it was so rare it hadn't even occurred to him.

No wonder she'd been sent back to earth under such vile circumstances this time. It all made sense now, even as he didn't want to believe it. The unsavory conditions of this life she was living, even before he came into it, were to be her final trial. To see if she could maintain her goodness under duress.

Had he been an idiot not to realize it? Damn. If he didn't take her now, she'd most likely move on to become one of them after this life cycle...or else she'd be given another go at life, since he'd pretty well sabotaged her this time. Or rejected altogether. Hell, anything could happen.

If she went to the ranks, she would be as the one sitting across from him now. His mortal enemy, both of them locked in an eternal struggle, mere instruments in this never-ending cosmic game.

He couldn't let that happen, but...

She would be so beautiful with her wings, it would pain him to look upon her. Another ache rose in the heart he hadn't thought he possessed until he met her.

The angel was waiting for his response to that bombshell. Keeping his expression vague—or, at least, hoping he did—Ash gave him a mocking smile. "Ah. So it all comes clear. Well, don't get your feathers in a ruffle. She's my sweet, scrumptious little candidate too. We'll take good care of her where she's going."

"I wonder if telling him that was the smartest move you could make," Nicolae said and, if Ash didn't know better, he would think the old man was scolding the angel.

"Yes, I know. He'll be even more determined now."

"I told you from the beginning how determined I was. I told you there would be no changing my mind. Whatever yoke you deem fit to strap on her in her afterlife makes no difference to me. She was signed over to me, and I intend to take her."

Nicolae turned to face him directly, not a hint of intimidation on his seamed face. "I must say, Madeleine's potential angelhood aside, I find the implications of your contract disturbing. If it's honored, it might set a precedent that could prove disastrous."

Ash sniffed. "And how's that?" he asked flatly.

"Well, once word gets around that any mortal on earth who's indifferent to another soul can damn that soul to Hell for personal gain, there could be chaos."

"Not any mortal. I didn't pull someone off the street. Gatlin was her father. He had claim on her himself, and he simply chose to relinquish it because he's a filthy bastard."

"He's not the only one," the angel muttered.

Nicolae ignored him. "All the same, we do frown upon these arrangements."

Ash sat forward, fighting the urge to leap out of his chair. He'd been halfheartedly thinking of a way to release Maddie himself, but he wanted it to be on his terms. His decision. If he was going to suffer punishment for losing a soul, he wanted it to be because he chose to. Not because he suffered a defeat. "Frown all you want. You aren't taking this away from me, damn you."

"Riam and I have been discussing it at length." So that was the angel's name. "We've found ourselves in a bit of a gray area, but we've reached what we feel is a fair compromise, and we were hoping you would be amenable. If not, then as the holder of the contract, you have the right to refuse. But with a potential angel at stake, Riam is prepared to take this matter to the High Tribunal, and I must say I'd be happy to refer it on."

Son of a bitch. The High Tribunal was supposedly neutral, like Nicolae, but it rarely turned out well for Ash's side.

"This isn't right. If she wasn't a Candidate, you wouldn't blink. What gives her more value than any other soul? The mere fact that you want to fit her with feathers and a friggin' gold halo and allow her to run amok spouting self-righteous bullshit? That's grand."

"Do you want to hear the terms of our compromise or not?" Riam demanded. "Because we can go straight to—"

"*Fine.* State the terms."

Nicolae gave one brief nod. "It's really quite simple. Offer her the same bargain."

"What?"

"It'll be her final trial of sorts," Riam said. "Only punctuated. Make her aware of what she's facing. Do whatever you must to be certain she fully believes you. Then tell her she has the option of naming another who can go to Hell in her stead."

"This is preposterous."

Riam was already talking over Ash's protest. "*If she does*

131

so, then your contract is in full force and she will be yours to do with whatever you wish. But you may only take her, not who she names."

"And if she doesn't name another?"

"Then your contract is null and void. You'll destroy it. You will no longer have any hold on her whatsoever. She will be completely free from you. She'll belong to us."

Ash felt a grin unfurl across his lips. "Impressive. If she tries to take the way out, she goes down. Such trickery even we rarely employ."

The angel scoffed. "I seriously doubt that. It's the only thing we could think of that you might agree to."

"I'm surprised *you* agree to it, that you aren't prepared to press the matter and try to get her released without putting her in such a predicament."

"Don't tempt me."

"No, really. You're that certain of victory, aren't you?"

"If she's truly fit for our ranks, and I'm convinced she is, then she will be that selfless. Yes."

"And if she's not, to Hell with her, quite literally. Right?" Ash chuckled. Riam only glared. "At any rate, it's an easy way to placate me, if I'll go along like a good little boy."

"Are you in agreement or not, demon? I could banter with you all day, but unfortunately I have scores of your kind's victims to contend with."

A vision of Madeleine's face rose in his thoughts, her blue eyes dancing as she looked at him. If he accepted the compromise, that meant he had to tell her what he was, what he'd done. Somehow it seemed far worse than the thought of taking her unaware. Inconceivable, almost. And if she tried to save herself, he had to be willing to watch her horror as she realized she'd just doomed herself.

He had to repress a growl and an outburst of furious frustration that might blow this house to pieces and hurtle Riam and Nicolae a hundred miles away. For the first time, he wished he'd never appeared in Gatlin's crappy, rat-infested apartment twenty-seven years ago. He almost wished he'd never set eyes on Madeleine. Or that he'd just taken her soul in the damn parking garage, or in the street, like he would have done if he hadn't been a colossal idiot. He wished he'd done it before he'd known her.

"Do we have an accord?" Riam asked.

It might still give him everything he wanted. Or he might lose her altogether.

One of his colleagues had been in love with an angel once. For centuries, he'd pined for her. When he'd tried to have her, finally, it had caused such an upheaval no one was certain whatever became of him. Ash wasn't prepared to go through that. He'd endured enough torment. He couldn't take any more.

It was only when the angel shifted uncomfortably that Ash realized he'd been staring dead at him, unmoving, for a good minute or so. With a snarled curse, he pushed himself out of his chair in a sudden burst of movement that made the other two flinch. Good. They were right to be afraid of him right now; he wanted to punch a hole in the world.

"We don't require your answer this very moment," Nicolae said calmly as Ash paced the length of the room like a caged beast, his hands clenching and unclenching at his sides. Given the way Riam's jaw tightened, he wasn't thrilled at the prospect of delaying the matter. "So long as you don't move to collect before you've given us your decision, of course."

No, he *had* to decide now—Metos would be after him yet again, wanting to know what the fuck was taking so long now that the stay was lifted. He'd be demanding Ash do whatever Nicolae asked to get their precious acquisition with as little hassle or outside interference as possible.

But he was beyond tossing back a scathing taunt at the other two. Indecision burned like flames licking at his skin. He wasn't accustomed to not seeing the way clearly before him. He'd wanted Madeleine, he'd gone after her. Part of him was screaming to refuse their compromise and face the High Tribunal, if that was what it took to claim her. The other part...

He didn't even want to consider the other part.

Dammit, if only he'd moved on her when things were simpler. How many times would he regret it? Now there was her memory to contend with. The softness of her skin. The silk of her hair. The sweet music of her laughter. Hell, the sound of his own. He'd lost this game when he'd given in to his desire to touch her. She'd beaten him.

All his thoughts came to a halt, and he ceased his relentless pacing. For that alone, for besting him without even trying, she deserved a chance to escape the fate he'd planned for her.

"Fine," he said to the two somber beings near the desk, and out of the corner of his eye he saw their heads lift and swivel toward him. But he couldn't bear to look directly at them as he spoke his agreement. "I'll give her the option. We'll see...how it goes."

Nicolae sat and began scribbling in his ledgers in his typical dismissive manner. Riam came to his feet and approached Ash, moving swiftly and noiselessly. Ash stiffened and cut him a warning glance that stopped him in his tracks.

"Don't say one gloating word to me, or I'll send you flying."

"I was actually going to thank you for being reasonable."

"That's almost as bad, coming from the one whose dirty

work I'm doing."

The damned angel laughed. "Are you actually mad at me for making you out to be *the bad guy*?" He shook his haloed head. "You demons are good for the occasional chuckle, I'll give you that."

Oh, he was so certain of his victory. It was all over his fucking face: the serenity, the smug triumph. Ash wanted to crack that expression, watch it fall piece by piece, if only for the fun of it.

He allowed a blithe smile of his own and strolled over to Riam until they were nearly nose to nose by the time he finished speaking. "One word of warning to you, before you get too busy patting yourself on the back, or stroking your own wings, or whatever it is you do to congratulate yourself. I can be...*extremely* convincing. I know terrors you can scarce conceive of, and I'll lay them out in such cruel detail for her that by the time I'm done, she'll damn every soul she knows to Hell if it'll save her own."

Grimness had slowly crept over Riam's face, lifting Ash's spirits considerably. Riam turned his head away, averting his gaze but refusing to step back.

"Then I suppose it's as you said, isn't it?" The angel sounded nowhere near as sprightly as he had a moment ago. "We'll see how it goes."

Tonight was the night. She knew Ash was going home tomorrow, and she'd been waiting for him to say *something* about what the future held. She could feel it when he held her, kissed her, when he made love to her—he wanted her. He *did*. She'd never felt such passion from any man she'd ever been with, and it only kept growing.

They had to talk about it tonight. If he didn't bring it up, then she would. She would be brave. She would tell him she wanted to see him again; she didn't care what that entailed. He could come here or she would gladly go to him. Delia had been dead-on in her assessment of the situation, and Maddie hated that she'd allowed it to come to this, to putting herself out there again when it always ended so badly. But Ash was a weakness, and he seemed so...different. Wasn't that the goal? To find the one who made you feel like no one else ever had, the one who seemed above all the petty game-playing?

And if he said that seeing her beyond tonight still wasn't what he wanted...oh God. It didn't bear thinking about. The thought of facing an empty bed every night after having him here was enough to spur her to action, even at the risk of a shattered heart. She slept so much more soundly with him here, with his arms around her. It was surely ridiculous, but she would swear that he really did keep the nightmares away.

She didn't need a life-long commitment—yet—but she needed the promise of more of him.

Maddie's heart jumped when the knock sounded at the door. She straightened the centerpiece on the dining table and gave the entire scene one final, critical survey. It wasn't much, but it looked nice. Soft candlelight glowed and the silverware gleamed. She hoped Ash liked lasagna. It was the only thing she knew how to make well.

Deep breath. Let it out. That done, she did a little pirouette toward the living room, gave her appearance a quick inspection at the mirror on the way and pulled open the door.

Somehow, impossibly, he was more gorgeous every time she saw him. He smiled at the sight of her and, unable to contain herself, she slipped through the door and into his arms.

But something was wrong, and she sensed it immediately.

He didn't crush her to him with his usual urgency, as if he were trying to fuse them into one being. He held back. Against her, he was stiff and distant.

Oh no. Don't let this go bad.

Quickly, she released him and stepped back, forcing a smile to her lips. "I'm glad you're here. Come on in, food's ready."

He followed her inside without comment, shutting the door behind him.

"It's just lasagna," she went on with determined optimism, heading to the kitchen. "I hope that's all right." Unfortunately— or fortunately, depending upon how one wanted to look at it— little of their time together had been spent going over likes and dislikes. And he was usually so vague about everything...

Maddie froze mid-step. It wasn't intentional—it was all of her thought processes shutting down in one moment of complete, blinding horror.

All this time, and she'd never asked him. Stupidly, she'd just assumed. How could she be so blind? The reluctance to share any information about himself, or to talk about seeing her again. The comment about bad timing. Hell, *everything*, every sign had pointed to a truth she'd refused to acknowledge. It was probably due to his uncanny ability to stop her midsentence and give her orgasms when she began to question too much— he'd kept her mind scrambled.

It was clear now. Her fingers gripped the edge of her kitchen island for a moment and then she whirled to face him, still holding on for support in case his answer wasn't what she wanted to hear. But her voice wasn't as demanding as she wanted it to be.

"Are you married?"

Puzzlement flickered across his face, and she wasn't sure

whether to be comforted by that or not. A lock of dark hair arced enticingly over his forehead. He was taking far too freaking long to answer, only looking at her in that disturbingly assessing way of his that raised the hair at her nape. As usual, her mouth ran away with her.

"I can't believe I never asked. I'm such an *idiot.* But if you're here and you've got a sweet wife at home taking care of a passel of kids or something, then I'm just...I'm just going to...oh God, I'm going to *hell.*"

He laughed then, the first utterance he'd given since arriving at her apartment. It was a tight, unhappy sound. "Well, Madeleine, I have good news and I have bad news. It's up to you which you want to hear first."

"I guess I'll delay the inevitable and take the good news."

"I'm not married."

She sagged in relief, one hand going to her wildly thumping heart. "Oh, thank God. You scared the crap out of me. Don't do that." Whatever bad news he had, at least she hadn't slept with some poor woman's husband. She wouldn't be able to live with herself. Once she'd caught her breath, she lifted her gaze to his, feeling the distance between them more than ever. "I suppose the bad news is that this isn't going to work for you, right?" Before he'd walked in her door, she'd been able to fool herself. But not now, with him standing in front of her. It was as if he'd brought in the truth and clubbed her over the head with it. "I know you know what I want. You have to realize I'd like to see you again, somehow. But I guess that isn't going to happen, huh?"

"It's not...anything like that. This—" he gave a gesture that seemed to encompass her and the entirety of her apartment, "—would work very well for me, actually. More than I'd like to admit."

"Oh. Well, then...what's the bad news?"

"I'm afraid the bad news is...there is a possibility that you could very well be going to hell."

Chapter Twelve

His voice cracked at the end, something that had never happened to him in all the eons he'd been contracting and reaping. It wasn't supposed to be hard. It was supposed to come naturally, but nothing since he'd touched Madeleine's soft white skin had felt natural. He felt as if his own skin were on inside out.

She wasn't taking him literally, of course. Confusion was written clearly across her furrowed brow. "What are you talking about? Did I do something?"

"You didn't do a thing. It's me. It's no one's fault but mine." It was true. Her bastard of a father should've been left to perish as he was meant to. Gatlin really couldn't be blamed for acting according to his own nature and saving himself. Ash turned away, unable to behold Madeleine's innocent puzzlement any longer.

An angel. They were right. She was an angel on earth right this moment.

"I don't understand. What's your fault?" Her voice didn't sound steady, either. At least he was in good company. "Look, I've heard 'it's not you, it's me' a dozen times. If you don't want to be with me, please do better than that."

"I want to be with you. The problem is that I wanted to be with you forever. And I can't, not without great cost to you."

"Okay, it's like you're speaking Swahili or something right now. I don't understand what you're telling me. Be straight, please."

By the Dark Lord, he didn't know how. He didn't *want* to scare her. He didn't want to show her those things he'd boasted about to Riam. It had all been talk. He was going to have to let her go. Everything on the inside of him felt twisted and contorted, out of place. Above all else, he didn't want to tell her what he'd tried to do to her. Riam and Nicolae had forced his hand, and he hated them for it.

"Madeleine, I'm not who you think I am. I'm not even what you think I am. The night you saw me for the first time was not the first time we've met."

"Okay," she said slowly. "Remember, I said I thought I knew you."

"Not the way you think. I've been following you all of your life, but you never saw me. I've been following you through...all your lives, and there have been many."

Her reaction wasn't what he expected. Her face smoothed over. Very calmly, she said, "What, like my guardian angel?"

"No. Just the opposite."

"The opposite. A...demon, then?"

She was patronizing him. She thought he was insane, or using this as some elaborate ploy to get rid of her. It was clear from the downturn of her mouth and that terrible, resigned coolness that had settled over her.

"Demon! Demon!" that stupid bird croaked excitedly from the bedroom. "All signs point to yes!"

"That's right. My name is Ashemnon. Twenty-seven years ago I entered an agreement with your father in which I could take his daughter—you—if only I would remove him from a situation that would result in his death. He traded you for his life, Madeleine, and now you belong to me."

"My father."

"Right."

"I don't even know my father."

"Irrelevant. He didn't know you, either. That didn't stop him. In fact, it probably made it easier."

"Tell me his name."

"Maxwell Gatlin."

He watched as all color drained from her face. Apparently she did know her father's name, but hadn't expected him to. For the first time, real fear began to creep across her features.

"You need to leave."

"I'm not going to."

Maddie left her sanctuary in the kitchen and all but sprinted toward the living room door. When he jumped in front of her to catch her, she was shaking. "I said you need to go!"

"I need you to believe me."

She fought his hold and full-blown panic gripped her when she found she couldn't break it, she couldn't even loosen it. "You're crazy. *Get out* before I start screaming."

Quick fix for that. One flick of his magic and time ground to a halt. "Think about it, Madeleine. All the bizarre things that have happened to you all your life, the nightmares, the frightening things you've seen. The constant dread you feel. You've told me about all of it, but I already knew. There *is* a dark entity around you. It's me."

Her eyes were huge and luminous, welling with tears that quivered and then spilled over her cheeks. "How could you use that against me right now?"

He stared down at her, doing little to conceal the power emanating from him, or the heat gathering behind his eyes. This was the moment he'd been dreading, but there was nothing to be done for it. He had to show her. And he watched in agony as understanding dawned in her gaze.

"It was *you* doing that to me? All this time I thought I was going crazy and it was *you!*" The last word was screamed, and she fought him with renewed strength, surging with all her might against him. *Fuck*, she believed him. He saw it. He wrapped her in his arms, knowing he should let her go, let her get as far away from him as she could. But he couldn't.

"Most of the things that happened to you were side effects of the claim on your soul. It wasn't anything I was doing to you directly, but it was still my fault. It amounted to a curse being placed on you. It was before I knew you, Madeleine."

"And that makes it okay? You ruined my life!" Another minute passed before she reached the end of her strength and her struggles gave out. She collapsed against him, sobbing noisily into his shirt while he stroked her hair.

"I thought it wouldn't matter if I knew you or not. I thought I would always be cold. But you did something to me, you made me feel. I know...you hate me," he went on softly, "and you have every right to. I want you to know that I'm done. I also want you to remember that no matter how hard your life gets, there are wonderful things in store for you. Things you can't even imagine. Just always do what you know in your heart is right."

Releasing her from his embrace was the last thing he wanted. What if he would never touch her again? That alone would be hell. Sighing, he let her go to pull the contract from the inside of his jacket. "This is all that's binding you to me. For me to destroy it...well, would mean some extremely harsh consequences for me. I don't care anymore, but now we have a way out. You've been given the opportunity to name someone else to take your place."

Alarm snapped her eyes wide open. "That's what I have to do to break it? But I can't do that."

He gripped her arm again. "Tell me that's your final decision." *Please.* It was the only way he could think of that she could be free and he just might escape his superiors' wrath with his life intact.

"I..." She trailed off, her eyes on the scroll still in his hand. He knew how it must sound for him to be urging her *not* to name a replacement. Like he still wanted her soul, when a moment ago he'd been telling her otherwise. Dammit.

"I don't know," she said, her voice small.

Always do what you know in your heart is right, Maddie. He stared deep into her eyes, willing the words to sink in. But all he saw reflecting from their limpid brightness was a rising malice that stunned him. It was coming from her thoughts too. He could feel it increasing in direct proportion to the quickening of her pulse rate.

"You said my father did this to me? And he's still alive?"

Grimly, he nodded. "From what I understand, after our encounter he turned his life around. He was on an express lane to Hell, trust me. But it's possible we've lost our hold on him."

Her lips twisted into a crooked, bitter line. "Do you want him back?"

"Madeleine. Think before you speak."

She covered her face with both hands, and he steered her to the couch. He wanted to pull her back into his arms, but she resisted his attempt, and he let her.

"I want to see him."

"For what?"

144

"I want to know *why*."

"I can tell you why. He was a drug addict like your mother. He was about to go down in a rain of gunfire. He'd never given a damn about anything except his next fix. It didn't take much to get him to cave in." He stroked her quivering back, expecting her to shrug him off, but needing more than anything to touch her. Despite the little shudders still racking her, she held still. "But the blame is solely on my shoulders. I should have left it alone. If you want to ask someone why, you need to ask me."

"All right." She turned to face him fully, her chin lifted in determination and her eyes still streaming but resolute. "Why? Why me?"

"First let me ask you something. Do you really believe me?"

"For as long as I can remember, I've thought there must be some reason, some explanation for the weird things that have happened to me. I would think you were crazy right now, or lying to me, except it all makes perfect sense. And thinking back on some of the things you've said and done..." She lifted a hand and wiped at her eyes. "I wouldn't believe you, I don't want to believe you...except that it's the answer I've been searching for all my life. Maybe it makes me a fool, but..."

"You're no fool. Quite the opposite. You were targeted because of your worthiness, Madeleine. That's how it works. I'd have done anything to claim you. I... No, that wasn't it. I was in love with you."

"So you would damn me?" The crack in her voice caused a fresh shard of pain to rip through him.

"To have you with me, yes. It didn't matter to me. I just knew that I wanted you."

"Because you'd known me in past lives."

He nodded. "Only the very best souls get to come back again and again. Most only get one go at it. You've been a

145

queen, a martyr, a philosopher—often you're a healer or philanthropist of some sort. It would explain the desire you were describing to me about being part of something bigger than yourself. You always have been."

"I'm sure not now," she said bitterly.

But you will be. Just wait. "I'm not asking for your forgiveness, I'm not even trying to make excuses or ask for your understanding. My own selfishness is the sole reason for what I did."

"And you're just going to let me go now?"

"It's not quite that simple. As I said, you have to name a replacement."

"Anyone?"

He hated himself, *detested* himself—along with Riam, Nicolae, all the world and the realms above and below—for having to lie to her yet again. But she would do the right thing. He knew she would. "As far as I know."

"What would happen to them?"

He sat back, tearing his gaze from her and fastening it on the thin hardback books resting on her coffee table. He'd wanted to rip her away from this world of normalcy. Take her to a place where she'd never hold a book again, never see flowers like the ones in the ornate vase on the end table next to her. Never again hear the music that was so dear to her.

And now he had to tell her exactly what he was, what he'd had planned for her.

"I would tear out their soul. I would kill them. And I would take them to Hell, which is every bit as bad as you've been led to believe all your life."

"Oh God." She stood up from the couch, her movements slow as she wandered a few paces away and stopped. She must be in shock. He supposed it wasn't every day a girl found out she'd been sleeping with a murderous, rampaging demon who'd set his sights on her soul next. "That's what you did to the guy who shot at us, isn't it?"

"Yes."

"I want you to go," she said without looking at him. "Please."

He got to his feet and stood behind her. "I need your answer, Madeleine."

"I *can't*," she sobbed, and the sound tore something loose inside him. "I can't do that to someone else. I can't do it to myself, either. I *hate* you for this. Please just go, I can't do this."

What if she didn't answer him? Would she be freed by default for refusing to name another? He was losing his touch, to neglect to get clarification on these matters.

"Whether you feel you can do it or not, it's upon you. You must decide."

She whirled to face him, her face as white as Riam's robes. "Don't make me say the words that will damn my soul, or anyone else's. I won't do it. I don't belong to you, dammit. I don't belong to anyone. No one had the right to do this to me, not even my piece-of-shit father. *I didn't ask for this!*" She stumbled backward as she screamed at him, and he feared she might trip over something and hurt herself. Everything she'd been holding inside all these years was flying out, and if he were mortal he'd fear for his own safety.

"Maddie, be careful."

"What do you care? You ruined what life I had and now you want to take eternity away from me too. I was falling in love with you!" She grabbed a picture frame off the table near her and hurled it at him. There was a cross hanging on the wall; she snatched it off and clutched it to her chest, triumph

147

suffusing her expression.

"That won't do any good, not to a contracted soul."

She threw it at him. He dodged it easily and turned slowly back to look at her. She had plastered her back to the wall behind her, and now she finally slid down it to crumple on the floor like a discarded rag doll. The carpet muffled her wild, racking sobs, but every one of them was like a dagger driving into his chest.

He couldn't do this anymore. The need to pick her up and comfort her and tell her he would never hurt her was too much to resist, but she would reject him. She would fight him and scream at him and possibly injure herself, and he didn't know what the hell to do.

As quietly as he could so as not to startle her, he knelt on the floor. The instinctive urge to touch her assailed him, but he beat it into submission. "Madeleine, I'll leave. All right? I'm not going to lay a hand on you. You don't have to answer right now."

Her sobs quieted, but she didn't lift her head.

"I don't want to hurt you. I didn't even want to scare you. All of that's in the past. Let me try to fix this. I'll do anything, everything I can to fix this. Please..." His voice gave out. He was about to ask her to trust him. How fucking laughable was that? Trust the monster who'd come to steal, kill and destroy her, who'd waited and stalked and bided his time until the moment she was most vulnerable. Because he'd been such a coward. "I'll find answers. Don't be afraid of me when I come back to tell you what I've learned. It's a necessity."

She picked her head up then, looking at him with half-blind, red-rimmed eyes. "What if you can't fix it? Are you going to take me? Can't you just let me go?"

When she looked at him with such pleading, spoke to him

148

in that broken voice, he wanted to rip the contract to pieces. Damn the consequences.

"I don't know." One moment longer they looked at each other, and then he stood. With barely leashed savagery, he strode to her door and scarcely resisted ripping it from its hinges as he slammed his way out. The air itself here was stifling him. He needed to go home, recharge, realign. Figure out what the hell he was going to do.

It wouldn't matter. He was fooling himself. He could spend a century prowling the caverns below with nothing but his tortured thoughts and he still wouldn't be any closer to a revelation about Maddie. He'd fucked up. That was what it all came down to. He'd fucked up and loved her.

Ash ceased his relentless pace and stood still in the middle of the parking lot of Madeleine's apartment building. His shields were still in place, so he threw his head back to the deepening twilight of the heavens and roared a single name.

"*Riam!*"

Maddie stared at her closed front door, still numb and trembling. She wanted to go to bed and never have to get up or face anyone else ever again. She'd gone from dating guys who left her to dating guys who wanted to kill her. She hated to think what was going to come around next.

It was thoughts like these that kept her sane, because she really couldn't deal. She couldn't. Ash was...evil. There had always been something a little odd about him, but...

Wiping her eyes, she made herself get up and lock the door. Get up and deal, the way she always did, even when she knew she couldn't. Carefully, she walked into her bathroom, fearing her legs might give out at any minute. The cold water she splashed on her face snapped her awake to the world again, but it was a world she didn't want to be in anymore. The reflection in the mirror was one she didn't even recognize. Pale skin, hollow eyes. Even her lips looked thin and compressed. Her hair was a mess from wallowing on the floor and on Ash's shirt.

A fresh wave of tears threatened as she ambled out of the bathroom into her bedroom. The sight of her bed, all neat and turned down and just waiting to be rumpled up, was almost her undoing. She'd hoped she and Ash would end up there tonight. She was getting damn tired of all her dreams being dashed on the rocks. Memories of them together assaulted her. How passionate he'd been. Had he been thinking of killing her even then? Taking her to Hell? Had he only been waiting for his moment?

He'd almost done it that first night.

She barely refrained from collapsing again at the thought. The mugger... Ash had put his hand on the man's chest, and the man had screamed and dropped. She remembered the weird feeling that had washed over her when Ash put his palm over her beating heart the first night they were together. She'd pulled his hand away and kissed it, and the sensation stopped.

God, she'd thought her love life was a disaster before. In a moment of melodrama, Delia had once announced that men were only good for murdering the soul. Ha.

Well, Dee, I've got one for you.

A blip of hysterical laughter escaped her lips. She couldn't call Dee. There was no one to turn to. No one she could go to with this. She was so alone. She'd never felt so alone.

"Riam!" Ash never thought he would ever in his entire existence call upon an angel's name. If the bastard didn't answer him...

"You called?"

He whipped around at the voice behind him to find Riam standing with his arms crossed, a quizzical expression on his normally serene face. "I want out of this."

The angel's eyebrows shot upward. "What?"

"I said I want out. I want this to just...go away."

"Then you have to break the contract."

"There isn't some buried-deep rule I don't know about that nullifies this thing without my interference? She's a potential angel, for fuck's sake. Surely you can pull some strings for one of your own."

Riam laughed, the asshole. "Trying to keep yourself out of hot water, as it were?"

"I don't want to overlook an easy solution."

"Right. Sorry, but no. She's not one of my own yet. If you want out, you have to break it. Only you."

That was as he'd feared, but it had been worth a shot. "I also wanted to ask what will happen to her. What have I done? Have I...ruined her chances?"

Riam pursed his lips and tilted his head back and forth, considering. "Probably not. It depends. I mean, I would have to get confirmation on that, of course. I'm not the final say on the matter. But she can't be held responsible for what you did to her."

Ash pulled out the contract. He ripped the black string and unfurled it, staring blindly at the words he once thought would give him everything he wanted.

"You love her," Riam said.

"How astute you are."

"Oh, I've known from the beginning. Ever since I was assigned this case and I wondered why you didn't take her from the moment she came of age. Then, every time we thought you were getting close, you pulled back. You gave her more time. Others who've been watching her throughout all her lives know how enamored you were of her. It doesn't take a scholar to see."

Ash glared at him. "You and Nicolae did this on purpose, didn't you? The whole two-week stay, pushing her into this decision...you knew all along I wouldn't follow through."

"Maybe." But Riam's smile gave up nothing.

"Fine, we've established I've been wonderful entertainment for all of you. I don't give a fuck. I just want to know she's going to be all right."

"She'll be perfectly fine. How could she not be? You'll be away from her."

It was the truth. He was the source of all her problems. But he didn't want to be, not anymore. He wanted to protect her. What if something happened to her and he was locked away rotting in some dungeon, unable to do anything about it? Or worse.

Ash closed his eyes and pushed out his next words by sheer force of will. "I need you...to promise me something."

"And that is?" the angel asked warily.

"I've never done this before. I don't know what's going to happen to me when I destroy it."

"They can't strike at her again. They've already tried that in the past, on another case. New rules were instituted to stop it from ever happening again. If you destroy that contract, she's free."

Ash nodded, more questions crowding on his lips. He couldn't seem to get them out, to ask for the angel's help.

"Well, if you want to ask me to watch over her...I'm sorry, I'm afraid I can't interfere personally. She'll make the choices to gain her wings or she won't. It's up to her."

"That's what I wanted to ask." He stroked the rough, thick parchment with his thumb, circling his own burnt-on initial. How he wished he could take it back. Or at least go back. He'd been so sure of things back then. He'd known who the hell he was.

"What I can do, though, is petition to place her under divine protection for a time. If it'll make you feel better."

"It would. Thank you."

"Well?" Riam asked after silent moments stretched out between them. "Are you going to do it?"

His masters were going to kill him if he did. He'd been trying to convince himself it wouldn't go to that extreme, but suddenly it was something he knew deep in the blackness of his own heart. The rule Riam had referenced assured it. To voluntarily release or even unintentionally lose a soul Hell needed would carry harsher penalties than ever before, because it was strictly forbidden to try to reclaim them.

There'd never been an easy way out of this. He probably would have faced death even if Madeleine had refused to name another, thus rendering the contract null and void. It still would have meant failure on his part.

Trembling, he grasped the contract at the top with both hands. Riam's brows dipped lower, a troubled furrow appearing in his forehead. "You would truly do this for her? Sacrifice yourself?"

Madeleine's face appeared in his mind, smiling at him. Beautiful. Then that face became lit with an ethereal glow, and snowy white wings spread beyond it. One of *them*, just as she was meant to be from the moment she was born. She would be the best of them.

"With all my heart," he said, and ripped the Gatlin contract in two.

Chapter Thirteen

Maddie came off the bed where she'd collapsed in tears, choking and gasping for breath. Oh God, what was this? She couldn't breathe, she couldn't...

As soon as the attack—whatever it was—had come upon her, it was gone. She filled her lungs with blessed air, expanding them to their max. If she could overflow them, she would, because the deeper she inhaled, the more a sense of peace she'd never known before seemed to seek out all the dark places in her soul and fill them up. Finally she couldn't take any more, and she exhaled slowly. That felt even better. Like all the bad things, the fear, the dread, were pouring out of her with every measure of breath she released.

Was she crazy? She couldn't be. Or if she was, it felt pretty damn good.

The gentle knock at the front door startled her. She scurried into the living room and peeked out to see Ash standing outside, his head down. As her heart knocked against her ribs, she saw him rub a hand hard over his face.

She didn't want to let him in. He hadn't been gone long at all, and that couldn't be good news, could it? But judging by the way she felt, *something* had happened. Leaving the chain in place, she cracked the door open. His head lifted, and she almost gasped at the frightening devastation on his face.

"What is it?" she asked, her voice trembling.

He gave her a smile. But it wasn't a heartening one, not in the least. "I just wanted you to know you're free. All is as it should be."

"They let me go?"

"I let you go." He went to turn away. "I hope you get everything out of life you wish, Madeleine."

"Wait!" She didn't know what made her do it, but she shut the door and disengaged the chain lock. Ash waited while she threw the door open wide again. "Where are you going?"

"Home."

"Oh. You mean..."

"Yes."

"Will I...ever see you again?"

He shook his head, as if he couldn't give voice to the answer. Her fingers went to her lips. Everything within her was crying out that it was a good thing, a very good thing. Except for the one little part that could tell by his face and the faint tremor he tried to hide by shoving his hands in his pockets that he'd given up more than she knew, more than he could tell her. Much more.

"I can't say I never meant to hurt you, Madeleine. There was a time when I did mean to. I had fun at your expense. But I realize now I never would have taken you. I couldn't." He reached out a hand toward her, paused and searched her face for reaction. She didn't move. Crazy though she might be, she craved his touch. A moment later, she had it. His hand cradled the side of her face; his thumb stroked her cheek. Wiping away the tear she hadn't realized had spilled. "I love you."

"Oh God. Ash..."

"If you ever felt the same, even for a moment, tell me now.

Tell me before I have to go."

She nodded. "I did. I loved you."

He accepted the past tense with good grace. It was all she could give him after everything she'd learned. But she slid her hand over his and held it there, unwilling for him to pull away. Not yet. "I feel so different. For the first time in my life, I feel like everything's going to be okay."

He nodded. "It is. Because for the first time in your life, or at least as long as you can remember, I won't be involved anymore. The curse is lifted. You're free."

"But you gave this to me, and you didn't have to."

His eyes went darker. "Don't make me out to be a hero. I've been nothing but a villain to you."

"Maybe you've spent so long telling yourself that, you can't think of yourself any other way. I've seen the good in you, Ash."

"You haven't seen half the evil."

Despite her grasping fingers, he pulled his hand away and stepped back. Her skin immediately missed his heat and tingled in the aftermath. She stepped outside her door to try to make up for the distance he'd placed between them. "Thank you, Madeleine."

"Don't go yet—"

She was talking to his back now. It was all she could do to keep her feet planted to the floor, to not run after him as he rounded the corner and took the stairs down to the parking lot. He obviously didn't want her to follow. *Please look back at me one more time, at least.*

He didn't.

They probably expected him to run, but he was done being

a coward. When he was around the corner of the building and safely out of sight of Madeleine's door, he stopped and stared down at the ground, willing the earth to claim him.

One look back at her and he might have run from his fate. Run straight into her arms and remained there until they were forced to come drag him home. But whatever they had in store for him, it would be a mercy. It would either take his mind off her, or it would kill him.

He felt the power rise around him, sucking at his feet, then his legs, rising into his torso and out to his fingertips. When it reached the top of his head, engulfing him fully, he'd be gone from this world, most likely for good.

He lifted his head and looked up at the sky, admiring the intricate patterns the bare limbs of the tree next to him made against the glittering black void of the sky. He wished that sky could be blue. The same color as Madeleine's eyes, eyes no longer darkened by the haunted shadow he had placed in them. Maddie belonged up there, beyond the clouds. Not where he was going. He'd done the right thing. He could take comfort in that much at least.

"Ashemnon."

Startled at the voice and a little alarmed as the invisible power slipped up over his mouth and nose—never his favorite part, the sensation had to be akin to drowning—he glanced over to see Riam standing next to the tree.

"Good luck to you," the angel said.

Ash managed to give him a nod. Then the creeping magic completed its journey and the earth cracked open to swallow him in a whirlwind of searing heat, screams and the sickly orange glow of the lake of fire.

"Ash!"

Madeleine flew around the corner of the building in the direction she'd seem him disappear. Back here there was a narrow passage between the apartments and an aging brown wooden fence. She'd expected to find him still walking along the carefully tended grass, but the only sound was the wind whistling through the limbs of a lone tree. There was an odd tinge of scent riding the sudden gust, something like...sulfur. It stung her nostrils. But there was no sign of him.

She pulled her sweater tight and glanced behind her. It was as if no one had been here. He was gone already.

She didn't know why she'd come. It was crazy, and she hadn't planned out what she wanted to say when she found him. But their exchange at her door hadn't satisfied her. They couldn't end this way. He deserved more than her pitiful words for giving her her life back, and dammit, she wanted to make him listen.

Giving her life *back* was inaccurate. Because of him she'd never had much of a life to start with. But it didn't matter.

She turned back around and shouted into the wind rushing through the alleyway, though its bite nearly stole her voice. "Ash!" Maybe she really hadn't been quick enough. Maybe he'd already reached the other end. She sprinted in that direction, halting when the alley opened into the courtyard.

It didn't make sense for him to come this way in the first place. It was time to face the truth: he'd said he had to go and he was gone.

A broken sob tore from her throat. "*No.*"

She had so many questions for him, and now there would never be any answers. She turned and began the trudge back to her apartment, silent tears slipping from her chin.

What happened then would remain a mystery for the rest of

her life. Something grabbed her out of nowhere, *something* knocked the air from her lungs with nothing but a single touch. Her body was wrenched to one side and slammed against the fence, and she found herself staring into the eyes of a man she'd never seen before. Big, golden-haired...and the most frightening thing she'd ever seen in her life with that killing hatred burning in his black eyes. As she stared in horror, they began to glow red.

Pain radiated from her chest, further cutting off her air and, when she tried to cry out, no sound would come. His hand shot out to grip her throat, the hold tightening to bone-crushing proportions. His other hand slammed into her chest and the agony there went nuclear, partially blinding her. Every nerve in her body screamed as if it were being torn out. But she knew, in the moment before the sudden rushing darkness could claim her completely, that it wasn't anything physical being torn out. It was her soul.

Ash, help me! He couldn't leave her now. He wouldn't.

She could no longer see, or feel, but she could hear. A sudden flutter like a thousand wings beating the air. An infuriated shout, an answering roar.

There was no strength in her; she could only assume she was lying on the ground by now. Judging from the direction the sounds were coming from, she was. She wondered if her heart even continued to beat. But it had to, didn't it? She was alive; she wasn't dead yet. The noises of a vicious fight were still swirling around her, close and then distant and then close again. Whoever they were, they seemed to be locked in a death-match.

Her muddled brain tried to make sense of the words tearing from their straining throats.

"You can't touch her soul. It is *written*—"

"I can still kill the whore."

"Kill her, and she goes with me. You've still lost."

Maddie tried to move and sensed...nothing. Numbness should be preferable to pain, only at the moment, it wasn't. It was infinitely more terrifying. She wasn't aware of the ground beneath her, of the blades of grass that should be prickling against her cheek.

What if she *was* dead? The voices coming from above her, arguing over her...they didn't sound like any voices she'd ever heard before. One of them was so clear and piercing it was almost painful—and she clung to that, because it was the only sensation she could discern in this tumult of darkness—but the other was low and menacing, a growl that couldn't have come from a human throat. The only thing she knew was neither of them was Ash, and she wanted him, needed him to come put a stop to this...

The noise from the fighting reached a crescendo. Maddie wanted nothing more than to get up and run away as fast as she could, but nothing on her body *worked*.

Paralyzed. Whatever he did to you, you're paralyzed.

After those words whispered through her half-functioning mind, all her thoughts became one repeated prayer.

Oh, please, God, help me...

Suddenly, absolute silence descended, and for one terrible instant she thought her hearing had gone too. But then she heard her name in that crystal, too-clear voice, sharp as wind chimes. It came from right above her.

"Madeleine?"

She couldn't reply. Would he think she was dead if she couldn't answer him? She found that, cold as she was, she could grow far colder and darkness could reach far deeper at the thought of those ramifications.

The voice grew softer, sighing. "Oh, Madeleine. I should have seen this coming."

What did that mean?

She wanted to weep from this frustration.

Riam stared down at the crumpled figure on the ground and wanted to drop through the earth and thrash every demon in Hell. Especially the one whose fault it was she was brought into this situation in the first place.

But his anger was short-lived. It turned out he'd lied to that one, assuring him everything would be all right. He had to gnaw his lip to keep from uttering a curse. After all these years, he should have learned not to overestimate the demons' ability to adhere to the rules. He'd been a fool.

Saklon, the coward who particularly enjoyed deeds such as this, had retreated back to the slimy, slithering depths from whence he'd come and left Riam with a colossal mess to clean up. Quickly, he surveyed the area to make sure Madeleine wasn't in danger of being found, then he stilled himself to send out the telepathic distress call to the earthbound angels of the area.

"This is Riam of the Order Iaoth, requesting aid for transport of a human female to the nearest safe house." He gave the address, though the angels were all aware of one another's locations and one of them should be able to find him easily.

A moment later, the answer came.

"This is Celeste. I'm en route, Riam. ETA fifteen minutes."

Good. If someone found Madeleine like this, she would be taken straight to a hospital. *Not* good. Kneeling next to her, he laid a hand upon her head and felt in one consuming rush the fear ripping her thoughts to shreds. Her soul was hanging on by mere threads. He could see it, like a vague, shimmery superimposition of herself overlaying her skin. Another second and she'd have been free of her mortal confines. He would've had no choice but to take her with him.

What choice did he have now? He couldn't put her back. But neither could he leave her this way, with one foot in her world and one in his. Maybe he should have let Saklon finish the job; at least then she would be free. But the horror of what had been going on right before his eyes had been too much for him to stand by and watch. He'd jumped to action without thinking.

"Madeleine, can you hear me? There's no need to speak. Think of what you want to say to me, and I'll hear it."

"What happened to me?" Even her mental voice was weak, wavering.

"I take it Ashemnon explained to you what he was, what he had planned for you?"

"Yes."

"That was one of his superiors who attacked you just now. He didn't succeed at killing you, but now you're...in between."

"What happens to me now? Where is Ash? Please, I need him."

"I'm sorry, Madeleine. I'll try to help you any way I can."

"Who are you?"

"My name is Riam."

"Are you...like Ash?"

"No. I'm the opposite."

"You're an angel?"

"Yes."

Worry lanced through the thoughts coming from her. She was wondering about the implications of the fact she was conversing with an angel. He stroked her head, knowing she couldn't feel it, but wishing he could soothe her somehow. He got the distinct impression that she didn't necessarily want to ask the question that formed in her mind then.

"Can I be saved?"

"That depends on your definition of salvation."

"Go back to the way I was before?"

Riam sighed. He didn't have any answers for her. "Just rest for now, Madeleine. You're safe. Someone is coming for you. Her name is Celeste. Trust her, she is like me, only confined to the earth. You won't be able to communicate with her like you can with me, but she'll take care of you."

A sharp blast of panic came from her. *"But...where are you going?"*

"I have to see what I can do to fix this. I'll remain here with you until she arrives. Just hold on."

She fell silent. What else could she do? She was completely at their mercy.

He wanted to tell her that, whatever happened, it would be all right in the end. Even if she couldn't go back to her former life, she was headed for much greater things. He doubted she would want to hear that right now. At the forefront of all her anguish was Ash. She wanted to know where he was, if he was all right.

Riam didn't address those concerns because he had absolutely no idea.

A few moments later, the glare of headlights swept briefly over the fence beside them and he glanced up to see a black SUV pull to the curb. The passenger side door popped open and

Celeste jumped out, casting a quick glance around before approaching them at a brisk pace.

She was looking well, dressed all in black and with her usually wild auburn hair tamed into a sleek, practical ponytail. Her gaze narrowed on Madeleine and her brow furrowed as she reached Riam's side. "Oh no."

He nodded, knowing she saw the same thing he did: Maddie's ghostly spirit clinging to her flesh. "Thanks for getting here so fast."

"How did this happen?"

"Can't you guess?" *"She's had her soul all but torn out by one of those fiends,"* he finished, pushing the thought over to Celeste. *"She's almost completely detached."*

"Riam...I don't mean to sound insensitive, but you should have let him finish the job. At least she wouldn't be suffering like this," she replied.

"I know," he muttered. It was nothing he hadn't already thought about himself. Still, it wouldn't have been the best solution to the problem, at least not in his mind. Madeleine wanted to live. She'd just been given her life back. She deserved the chance to enjoy it. He wanted her to have it.

It wasn't in an angel's power to kill a human, so freeing her himself was not an option. He didn't know what to do.

"Which one did it?" Celeste asked.

"Saklon," another voice said, almost spitting the word out. "I can still smell the bastard." Riam turned to see Damael, Celeste's lover, stride up behind them. He went directly to Madeleine, bent and lifted her in his arms, cradling her against his chest like a sleeping child. "We can talk later. Now we have to get her out of here before someone sees."

Riam stood rooted in surprise. Damael was a former demon

himself, turned mortal by the angels in exchange for saving Celeste's life after almost killing her by accident. It wasn't that Riam was *uncomfortable* with him here, exactly, but...it was still jarring. He didn't think Damael had exactly joined their side, or was sympathetic to their cause at all. "I wasn't expecting you," he said as they quickly made their way back to the waiting vehicle.

Damael climbed into the back of the SUV with Madeleine as Celeste held the door for him. Once he was settled, he turned a smirk on Riam. "Anything for a little excitement on this big ball of mud."

"Oh, please," Celeste said, amusement tingeing her voice even as she ran around to get behind the wheel. "As if you don't get plenty of excitement."

"Only from you, my lovely one."

"Take care of her," Riam said, and Damael turned his unsettling black gaze back on him. Sympathetic to their cause or no, Celeste trusted him. So Riam had to trust him too.

"I will," he said, serious for one rare moment. He looked down into Madeleine's face. "I know who she is."

"Of course you do," Riam said, unable to keep the bitter derision out of his voice. "She's been a target for your kind for ages, hasn't she?"

"Not my kind anymore," Damael shot back. His eyes reminded Riam of a viper about to strike. "Let's not forget that. I'm not planning to serve her up to Saklon on a platter. I have as much reason to hate him as any one of you, and he has just as much reason to kill me. But it happens Ashemnon was a friend of mine, and any fool could see he loved her."

"What do *you* suggest we do?" Riam asked.

"Well, you can't help her. And Celeste and I can't, obviously. But a demon can."

"What?"

"Ironic, isn't it? You probably don't know this because use of the power is virtually unheard of. But it happens they can return what's been taken—well, within a reasonable amount of time. But she hasn't been taken at all—her soul is still here, if what you say is true. It can be reattached...if a demon is so inclined to reattach it."

Riam only stared, his mind firing. Damael narrowed his eyes on him. "So if you want to help her without killing her, your mission is to find the only demon in Hell who is."

Chapter Fourteen

He didn't know how long he'd been here. Apparently, they thought the blissful black oblivion of nonexistence was too good for him, so he was here, trapped, chained. Knowing exactly what they'd tried to do to Madeleine the moment he'd returned, but not knowing what had become of her.

"How are we doing today, Ashemnon?" The voice he hated beyond all reason hissed near his ear. He didn't know who this sadistic bastard was who doled out his torture—the metal mask on his face was solid, robbing him of sight—but he wished he could get his hands on him just once. Blinding agony seared his side, something sharp and burning, and all his limbs wrenched against their restraints. But he refused to utter a sound, gritting his teeth until they nearly broke.

"So stoic, aren't we? I wonder how your whore is doing? If I went to the surface, do you think she'd treat me as sweetly as she did you? I'm sure she would. After all, she can't move, she can't fight. She can't even scream. We could all take turns—"

The words robbed him of all reason, enraged him more than physical pain ever could. "Mother*fucker*, you'd better hope I never get out of here."

A cruel laugh. More pain. Caught off guard in the anguish of the imagery his tormenter's words had incited, he roared, fighting the chains that bound him. They only bit deeper. "Get out of here? Laughable. As for her—can you imagine how frightened she is right now? She'll slowly waste away, you know, waiting for you to come save her...it would bring a tear to the eye of a true romantic. That's what you are now, isn't it? Are there tears in your eyes right now, Ash? Maybe I should gouge them out for you."

Riam, Ash thought. Riam wouldn't let her suffer. He wouldn't abandon her—he would figure something out. As much as Ash had hated him, insulted him, the angel was shrewd. Even if Madeleine had to...had to die, she would be all right, because she would go with him. But he could hardly bear to think about the possibility. She didn't deserve that—she deserved the life she'd never been allowed to have because of him.

Knowing she was up there, hurt and afraid, was all that was keeping him sane right now. That was good, even the pain was good. It kept him sharp. He had to keep his wits about him if he was going to find a way to help her.

"Enough," a voice stated, and the agony stopped. If Ash hadn't been half hanging from the ceiling, he would have collapsed to the floor. The chains nearly crushed his wrists as they took the brunt of his weight. The voice he'd heard belonged to Metos.

"Where the fuck have you been? Can't bring yourself to come down here and see what you've done?" Dammit, it was frustrating not being able to see who he was talking to. He'd never felt so fucking powerless. Never.

"Ash, I have orders to follow, same as you. I don't follow them, I end up right here beside you."

"What a shame that would be."

"I didn't do this to you. You brought this all on yourself."

"Fuck you. You don't know what I've been through."

Metos gave a short bark of laughter. "What you've *been* through? By my watch, all you've been through for the past two weeks is that woman's bed. I realize the angel's stay was granted, but had you moved earlier, that wouldn't have been an issue. Oh no, you had your head in the clouds, you let her get to you. I worried about you, but I thought surely you would come through in the end. You didn't. You let that winged rat make a fool of you, of us, and we cannot abide that."

"I don't give a shit how big a fool you look. Nor myself any longer."

"It truly saddens me that it's come to this. That you've come to this. You were once great."

Great? He'd never been great. He'd been terrible, feared, even worshipped. But he'd never been great until he'd been in Madeleine's arms. The only true greatness he'd ever achieved was ripping that contract in two—now if only he could figure out a way to undo the consequences of that action for her.

"Metos, please. I once considered you friend. If ever you felt the same for me, you have to let me go. Let me help her. She's not ours any longer, so what does it matter to you if she lives?"

His superior's voice had never been warm during this exchange, but now it turned so cold and brittle it could've cracked and melted on the scorched fumes. "It matters to me because you'll be far more tormented by knowing she suffered, died and is beyond your reach forever. Once she's gone, I might even recommend releasing you. See if you can't try to rebuild what she tore away from you."

Yeah, release me. You do that. He kept his mouth firmly closed on that thought. Unfortunately, Metos couldn't seem to do the same. "Your punishment here isn't only for releasing a contracted soul. Your punishment is for being so fucking *stupid* as to fall in love with one of them. We've been through this once. We aren't going through it again."

"All right." Now that there was a glimmer of hope, he would switch strategies. He would keep his mouth shut, he would hold the threats in. They would finally let him go and he would rampage his way to Heaven to find Madeleine, if he had to. Even if it killed him. "All right, I hear you. I was stupid. Do you think I don't see that now? I knew all along I should've acted sooner. I'll take my punishment quietly if you'll just let me go when...when the time comes."

Metos grunted, not sounding convinced. "We'll see about that. It's an idea, not a certainty." There was the sound of footsteps heading away from him. "I take my leave now. Continue."

Continue— Oh, that bastard. Ash heard the sadistic chuckle of his tormentor as the slimy piece of shit stepped up to him again. "Miss me?"

"Like I miss your mother." It made no sense, but Ash made a point of laughing uproariously. Fuckers weren't going to break him as easily as they thought.

"I'm going to carve my name across your chest."

"Make sure you spell it right. If you can." He set his teeth against the anguish he knew was soon to follow.

Time could be deceptive here. Hours could feel like days, or conversely, days could pass in only a few minutes. He hoped not much time had gone by, because every minute counted for Madeleine. But his hope was running out.

"How long have I been here?" he finally asked his constant companion, drooping against the cursed chains that kept him from falling to the ground. His voice sounded too weak to his own ears.

"What makes you think I'd tell you that?" The sound of metal scraping against metal grated in Ash's head. What was he bringing out now? Fuck, if only he could *see*...

Or maybe his lack of sight was a blessing. The other demon could very well be bringing out the rack—or worse—now that Ash was weak enough that he wouldn't be able to fight them when they placed him in it.

The magic holding him in human form had long since fallen away. If Madeleine had been standing here now, she'd see a beast she would run screaming from. Maybe even more so now that his wings were in tatters and he could tell he was encrusted with grime and blood that ran black. His clawed hands clenched into fists. *Madeleine.* He was going to lose her, might have already lost her.

That knowledge, not the fear of any impending torture, gave him a surge of furious energy. He jerked against the chains, roaring and cursing.

"Well, well, he's showing spirit again. I like it. Gives me something to break all over again. Along with his bones."

Someone else was here; he heard their feet shuffling. Felt hands first on one arm and then the other, working at the chains. This could be his chance if only the damned mask weren't still in place. It had become so heavy he could hardly lift his head. He had no way to remove it. Still, he prepared to give them a hell of a fight.

It didn't last long. As soon as his limbs were free, he hit the floor after only a few pathetic struggles. The others' laughter echoed throughout the room. Then their hands were on him again, lifting him, placing him on the dreaded contraption.

He wouldn't beg, wouldn't give them that satisfaction. But he did discover, when he felt his hands being tied down, that demons could pray. They could do it fervently.

And even have those prayers answered, somehow.

"*Stop!*"

Ash must finally be hallucinating, because that voice wasn't whose he thought it was. It couldn't be. It had made him cringe far too many times to be welcome now...but it was. Holy fuck, was it ever welcome.

"Riam?" he said and, if indeed he was imagining things, then the others were too, because they emitted vicious hisses at the intrusion of an angel in their quarters. Ash could almost laugh at the way Riam must look right now, all bedecked in pristine white and gold amidst the darkness and squalor of the dungeon. But he was too stunned for anything other than a silent *thank you* to whoever had been listening.

"I have an order from the High Tribunal that he is to be released at once."

"Let him go." That was Metos, his grim voice coming from somewhere near the entrance. "But I'll have you know this isn't over, angel."

"It is for now." Riam seemed to be walking closer as he spoke. "Get him out of this cursed thing this *instant.*"

A moment later, Ash's hands were free, and he was lifted upright. Fingers fumbled at the back of his neck, unfastening the lock on the mask, and it fell away. By all that was unholy, it felt good. He groaned, rolling his head on his shoulders, before finally cracking open his eyes.

Riam's brightness caused him to screw them shut again. He hadn't realized how blinding that bastard was up on the surface. The hands that had been holding him up pitched him forward. He expected to land in a humiliated heap on the floor, but instead, strong arms caught him under the shoulders. Silken robes brushed his face, and the welcome scent of the topside world filled his nostrils, chasing out the bitter, burning sulfur.

"Thank you," he said, unable to lift his voice above a whisper. His eyes opened just enough to see that inches from his face, one of the protective amulets burned orange and flickered like fire where it hung around Riam's neck. It was the only way the angel could survive in this atmosphere.

As usual, Riam was all business. "Madeleine needs your help. Are you willing to accept mine to go to her?"

"With all that's within me, yes."

Metos's voice from across the room was like the crack of a whip, something else he'd grown accustomed to while he'd been in this hole. "You leave here to go to her and you die, Ashemnon. I'm done with this. You'll face the slowest and most agonizing death you can imagine."

Riam ignored him. "And you *will* help her?"

"You even have to ask me that?"

"Yes, I do."

"I'll do anything for her. I'd gladly let you put me back on the rack if only it would save her."

He sensed the angel nod. "That's good. But there is one other promise I need you to make me before we do this. It's very important."

"*Anything.*"

Riam hoisted him up as best he could and began trudging toward the entrance with him. "Don't let her see you looking like this. My God, you're ugly."

Chapter Fifteen

Madeleine didn't know how much time had passed and, since Riam had left, she had no one to ask. It had to be days, surely. *Surely.* Every minute that ticked by brought her closer to someone coming to save her, so she had to believe something would happen any moment now. It was the only thing keeping her going.

Except Celeste. The other girl stayed and talked to her to keep her company. She came up with idle chitchat as best she could with no response, and sometimes she read to her. From what Maddie had been told, there was a network of angels on earth and she was in one of the many houses they owned. She was lying in a bed, according to Celeste, and should be comfortable.

Every so often a man came in and spoke with Celeste—she recognized his voice as the one who'd been with her and Riam when they'd come to Maddie's rescue. They called him Damael and he had to be Celeste's boyfriend or husband, judging from the way they flirted. They were obviously in love. Just before Riam had left, Maddie had asked him to get someone to go to her apartment and take care of her parrot. Damael offered to do it, and she'd overheard the hilarious conversation that ensued when he got back.

"That bird called me a demon!"

"*What?*" Celeste had asked incredulously.

"It freaked me the fuck out."

"I bet." Celeste had laughed and laughed. "I'll go with you next time. I've got to meet this bird."

It was hard to lie there and listen to people talk about something she could easily clear up. But that exchange had given her some amusement. So did a lot of the other things Damael said. He had a wry wit that reminded her a lot of Ash, which only made her miss him all the more.

Floating in pitch-black nothingness gave one a lot of time to ponder life's quandaries. Everything had happened so fast—one day she'd been dating what she thought was a normal guy, the next day she'd learned he was a creature from Hell who wanted her soul. What would tomorrow bring, if she ever got out of here? She wanted to find out. So many times in life, she'd wondered if there was a point to it all. But there'd been a curse on her, and it was lifted now. She'd never been so eager to simply *live*, and her heart broke to think she might not get a chance to. How long could she stay this way and survive?

At that moment, she was alone, but she thought she heard movement outside the room. No, more than that. She heard shouting.

Fear shot through her. What was this, now? Another attack? She still feared one of them would come back to finish what they'd started, though Celeste had assured her she was safe and well protected. The door to her room flew open, banging against the wall, and if she could've scrambled from the bed and hidden under it, she would have.

"Maddie!" Celeste's voice was high and excited, no hint of fear. "Riam's back! He's brought Ash."

Oh, thank you, God. Thank you. The irony of thanking God for her demon lover wasn't lost on her, but she couldn't worry about it at the moment.

"Madeleine." That voice, *his* voice, Ash's voice... Deep in her soul, she cried just from hearing it again, but he didn't sound right. Frustration ate her alive and she mentally screamed out to the only one who could hear her.

"Riam! Is he okay?"

"He's fine. He's weakened, but he's okay."

"Please, please tell him to hold my hand."

She heard him sigh in her mind. *"He already is, sweetheart. Like he's never going to let it go again."*

"Tell him I love him."

"Wait a moment and you can tell him yourself," Riam said out loud.

"I'm here," Ash whispered, so close his lips had to be pressed to her ear. Everything within her wanted to surge toward him, feel his strength. And if he was weak, she would lend him what she had left. "It's going to be all right, Madeleine. I'm going to fix this."

Dammit, he needed to hurry because she had so much to tell him. He didn't have to bother saying he would help her—she knew he would. No matter what he'd said at her door just before this nightmare had gotten infinitely worse, she knew better. Maybe she shouldn't forgive him for what he'd done to her. Maybe she was crazy for doing so. All she knew was that most of the time she'd lain here helpless had been spent worrying as much about him as about herself. She was more than willing to find out what that meant for them, if he felt the same.

Ash squeezed her hand. It was when she returned the gesture that she realized she'd felt him do it and had even felt her own response. Excitement rang through her, and the muscles in her legs jerked.

"Easy," Ash said. "Just relax, let it work." Now she could feel his palm resting on her chest, just as he'd done their first night together. Only now, instead of pulling the life from her, he was giving it back. Warmth radiated out from his hand, stealing through her limbs. Bringing rush after rush of sensation, so unfamiliar now it was almost painful. She inhaled and felt her lungs expand. Oh, it was glorious to *feel* again. But nowhere near as glorious as it would be when she could see his face.

Ash watched her, trembling under the exertion of the spell. He was thankful he had the strength to do it at all. The fatigue was nothing that wouldn't take care of itself in time, but he needed to be strong for her *now*. And he would be, no matter what it took out of him.

When her eyes slowly opened, he wanted to collapse in relief...until she focused on Riam standing at the foot of her bed.

"Wow," she breathed, seemingly transfixed. Too transfixed. Ash glanced back and really noticed what Madeleine was seeing for the first time: Riam with his broad chest, flowing black hair, snowy white wings and sky-blue eyes.

"Hey!" Ash protested. Madeleine looked at him then—*finally*—and her face broke into a big grin. Her eyes filled with tears. It was all the confirmation he needed.

"Hi," she whispered. She held out her arms and he went into them, pulling her up off the bed. He stroked her hair as she sobbed quietly into his shoulder. "I love you, Ash. I was so afraid I'd lost my chance to tell you that I really do love you."

Burying his face in her hair, he rocked her, soothed her, murmured his love for her in return. Riam had moved away and was very softly conversing with Celeste and Damael in the far corner of the room. Ash had been so stunned to see his old friend here, Damael had laughed riotously at the look on his face. And Ash hadn't been able to verbalize what it meant to him: that seeing Damael here and happy with the woman he loved had given him more hope than anything had in his entire existence. Even more than that damn crazy angel appearing as if by magic in his torture chamber.

But hope was a short-lived thing. No one had said anything about freeing him; they'd only allowed him to come to the surface to help Madeleine. He didn't have the heart to tell her right now that he couldn't stay with her.

It never would've worked anyway, because of what he was. All he could hope for was to find some way to survive, and maybe one day, ages from now, he would get to see her in all her angelic splendor. He would live for that day.

Maddie drew away from him, holding his face with both hands. She kissed him, her sweetness a balm to his weary, pain-riddled body. What he wouldn't give to take her home, spend a few hours in her arms letting her put him back together again. Maybe Riam would allow him that much. It wasn't as if he had anywhere to run.

"There are too many people—or whatever—in this room," she said impishly against his lips. Apparently she was having the same ideas as he. "Can we go home now?"

"Madeleine...I wish it were that simple."

Her limpid blue eyes searched his. A single tear trembled on her bottom eyelashes. "What do you mean?"

"I was only brought here to help you. I can't..."

The tear spilled. Her expression shattered. "What? *No.*"

"Shh. You know it's for the best."

"But it isn't. It isn't the best for *me*. There has to be

someone I can talk to or—"

"No, I'm afraid that isn't possible."

"Ash, you can't leave me. We have to try anything. Do you want to stay?"

He could lie, tell her he didn't. It would break her heart, but maybe it would put any outlandish ideas out of her head. In the end, he couldn't say the words. There'd been too many lies between them, and he never wanted to speak anything other than the truth to her again.

"More than anything, angel. But I can't. There isn't anything to be done about it."

There was a sound at his back, and Ash turned to see Riam standing just behind him. "I'm afraid it's time to go."

Ash nodded, disentangling himself from Madeleine's arms. It felt like leaving a limb behind. "I'm ready."

"You can't take him away from me!" Madeleine burst out, her sudden devastated fury focused all on the angel.

"Maddie, it's going to be all right—" Ash began, but Riam cut him off.

"The order was only good for him to save your life, Madeleine. Whatever punishment his masters see fit to dole out, it still stands. The Tribunal won't get involved in that."

"Why not? It sounds to me like they can do whatever they want!" she fired back. "Please, Riam—"

"It's not my decision to make."

"But you talked them into this much. Surely you can do something."

"What I can't do is disobey their orders, which state I'm to return him once you have been restored. It's been done."

Her voice cracked on her next words. "No it hasn't. I'm not *restored*." She dissolved into sobs.

Quietly, Ash pulled her head to his chest and looked up at Riam. "Can you give us a few minutes alone?"

Riam's mouth thinned with uncertainty, but he finally gave a curt nod and walked from the room, warning them he would be just outside the door. Damael and Celeste followed, their expressions grim.

"Madeleine," Ash murmured, trying to get through to her over her racking sobs. They were so severe she could hardly breathe around them. "Listen to me. You're going to get over this. You're going to leave here and get on with your life, and things are going to be a whole lot better for you than they ever have been. Forget about me and live your life."

Somehow, words formed from the hiccups tearing from her throat, but he thought surely he misunderstood them. "You should have done it."

"Done what?"

"You should have taken me when you had the chance. You wouldn't be in all this trouble, and I could be with you."

The statement sparked such a vile reaction in him, he had her face in his hands and her head tilted back before he realized it. She gave a tiny gasp as his gaze bored into hers, and he spoke with such emphasis that each word shook her. "Don't say that. Don't even think that. Everything that's happened here today, everything we've done, was to keep you safe."

"I don't care."

"Yes, you do. You're irrational."

"I don't care," she repeated, practically snarling at him. "Don't tell me I'm fucking irrational when for the first time in my life, I know exactly what I want and where I belong. That's with you, wherever I have to go. I want you. Take me." Her hands slithered up over his shoulder, fingers kneading.

Aghast at her determination and the dark, violent passion it stirred in him, he fought the urge to leap off the bed and put as much distance between them as possible. She'd just handed him her soul on a platter, after everything he'd gone through to let it go.

"You don't know what you're saying," he hissed, but his hands weren't making any move to release her. Cold blackness welled up inside him, a chilling void that would draw her into it if he didn't keep it in check. "You have no idea what you'll be giving up."

"I'll be giving you up if I stay and that's too much."

"Has Riam told you that you could have the chance to be like him someday? An angel. Madeleine, think about it. Everything you've done, every life you've lived, all the good things you've done, all the pain and the trials—every bit of it has been leading up to that. To what you told me you wanted, to being a part of something bigger than yourself."

"Maybe it's all been leading up to you."

His breath hitched, stuttered and stopped. "It's out of the question." The words strangled him. With a sudden burst of effort, he shoved her hands away from him and stood, pacing away from the bed to stare out the window. Outside, it was a picturesque spring morning. Inside, he felt as if all of winter collected in his heart.

There was a rustle behind him, and he turned to see Madeleine on her feet, toddling toward the door. "What are you doing? You should rest."

"I'm fine."

He moved to get in front of her and guide her back to her bed, but she shoved at him with a strength that surprised him. "Get out of my way."

"Where the fuck are you going?"

"I'm going to talk to Riam."

Oh, hellfire, that would spell disaster. "That isn't...advisable at the moment."

"It's advisable for you to get the hell out of my way, Ash. I've been a pawn in your little game *my entire life*. Do you realize that? And now you're going to stand there and make this decision for me? I won't have it."

He could only stand and watch as this little mortal woman defeated him. Again. She pushed past him, staggering on her unsteady feet but throwing off any of his attempts to help her. He could only follow her into the hallway, and stand uselessly behind her as she caught the attention of the angel who'd been talking to Celeste.

Riam frowned as he saw her. "You should—"

"No, I shouldn't. I want you to know that if Ash has to go back to Hell, then I go too."

"*Madeleine!*" both Celeste and Riam snapped, as if they were shocked parents dealing with an unruly teenager. Riam's gaze whipped up over her shoulder, connecting with Ash's and glowing impossibly blue. "This is your idea of helping the situation? You son of a—"

"Hey, don't look at me. This is all her."

"Because you've poisoned her mind!"

"For the first time in my life, my mind is absolutely clear. But is it true what he just told me?" she asked. "He said I could become like you someday."

Riam's glare sharpened, if that were even possible. "Ordinarily the Candidates are never told that they're—"

"See, that's my problem with this whole thing. All this secrecy, all this planning and plotting I'm utterly unaware of. Is it that way with everyone? Is this all just a big game between the two of you, an eternal power struggle? Is that the meaning of life?" She scoffed. "Then I don't care about living anymore. I don't care about being one of you and perpetuating the cycle. I just want to make my own decision, and I choose to be with him. I love him. And I know he loves me just because I know what he was willing to give up for me. You can't tell me there was anything *poisonous* about it."

"I was standing there when they said he was as good as dead if he came to help you. If you go and they kill him, Madeleine, you'll be alone and in more misery than—"

"If I stay here, I'll be alone and in misery. If I go, maybe they'll spare him. This was all about me in the first place, wasn't it? It can only help if he delivers me like he was supposed to."

"The problem with your logic is you're forgetting who you're dealing with."

"No, I'm not. I'm standing right next to one of them."

"She's got a point there," Celeste said, looking none too happy about Riam's last statement.

Ash had scarcely been able to breathe through this exchange. Riam had lost most of his animosity while watching Madeleine's tirade, and he stared at her now with increasing heartbreak. After a long, silent moment, he looked back up at Ash. "She's declared her wishes. She's yours. It's up to you."

Gently, Ash took her shoulders and turned her to face him. "Madeleine—I can't take you away from the sunlight and this world you love. The people you love. Don't ask me to do it."

"Is it really that bad?"

"Yes," three voices chorused at once.

"But I'm used to it," Ash added. "You're not."

Her lower lip quivered. "I won't get used to it in time?"

184

He stared at her, considering. Who was to say? With him at her side—if he could stay at her side and not meet a grisly end—she might glory in the darkness. He thought of that first night in her apartment, staring down at her in her bed, at her face split by light from the window. Half in light, half in shadow. Each equally beautiful. Madeleine had as much darkness in her as she had light. Maybe he'd been the one to put it there, but it was a part of her now and she would carry it with her always.

Maybe it's all been leading up to you.

"I want you to think about it," he said. "I don't want you to make any hasty decisions you'll regret."

"And you'll regret this one," Riam grumbled.

"Hey," Celeste said, giving Riam's arm a shove. "You've said your piece. Thank you. But you haven't thought to ask the opinion of the one who did give up everything for one of them."

Riam gave a sweep of his arm as if to indicate the floor was all hers, then turned his back, pacing a few steps away.

"Look," Celeste said, taking Madeleine's hands. "When they stripped my wings and cast me to earth for loving a demon, they might as well have sent me to Hell for the shock of it. Simply having a mortal body hurt like I can't describe. I came to earth often before that, but fitting in to life here was another matter entirely. For a long time I was alone. I didn't have Damael, but he haunted my every moment, waking or sleeping. When I finally saw him again—it made it all worth it. Do I wish things could be different? Yes, of course. But would I do it all again?" She smiled. "In a heartbeat. For him."

"Thank you," Madeleine said quietly, a calm settling over her features as if this was the confirmation she'd been waiting for.

"I want you to think about it too," Celeste said. "In the end, I didn't have a choice, but you do. I can't say what you'll be

185

facing if you go there." She eyed Ash warily. "I'd be very careful, if I were you."

"You don't even have to tell me." He was actually considering this, then. If he was honest with himself, he'd know he'd been considering it from the moment she suggested it. Rubbing a hand over Madeleine's shoulder, he said, "It's you I'm worried about. If you end up there alone..."

"Ash, you were willing to sacrifice yourself for me. How would I be worthy of that if I'm not willing to do the same thing for you?"

She wanted to be worthy—of *him*? What backward alternate universe had Riam dropped him into? He couldn't speak; he could only look at her, her earnest blue eyes and soft, trembling mouth. Look at her and know he could never be without her as long as he was alive.

"I have an idea," he said, but he was speaking more to Riam's back than to anyone else. Seeming to sense that, the angel turned around. "But I need your help."

Chapter Sixteen

Night fell. Madeleine stood alone on the balcony outside the bedroom she'd been given, looking up at the stars. A light *ahem* behind her turned her head. Riam lent his otherworldly glow to the darkness as he stepped out and joined her at the railing. She smiled at him and went on perusing the stars.

"This is absolutely what you want?" he asked.

"I just want him."

"I think he has a good idea, giving you a glimpse of what you're in for before you commit...but I wish I could change your mind about the whole thing."

"You can't."

"Oh, I know." He sighed. "You'd have been a force to reckon with, Madeleine. I'd have loved to have seen you wearing wings someday. I think you'd have made every demon in Hell tremble."

"I doubt that."

"I don't."

They spent a moment in silence. Madeleine closed her eyes as a breeze grazed her cheeks, and she pulled her light sweater closer. In a moment, Ash was going to drag the soul from her body as Saklon had tried to do. As she'd seen Ash himself do to someone else. Her heart thudded dully and a fine tremor shook her that had nothing to do with the wind's chill. Earlier she hadn't been afraid...and she still wasn't. Exactly. She was simply apprehensive, she decided. She'd have thought she would have been terrified.

"There's not a chance of that happening for me if I do this, huh?" she asked quietly.

He shook his head. "Ask Celeste what happens to angels who fall in love with demons. We can forgive a lot, but not that. I'd hoped once you learned what he was, what he'd done, you would hate him."

She wanted to tell him she found that pretty fucked up. But she bit down on the words. Riam didn't have to help them tonight—he could have escorted Ash straight back to Hell as he was supposed to. Despite his position on the demons, he'd agreed to give this crazy scheme of theirs a shot.

"You wouldn't happen to be a bit of a hopeless romantic yourself, would you?" she teased.

He chuckled. "Not at all. I leave that to the fickle mortal heart."

"Oh, so I'm fickle?"

"No, not you. Obviously not."

She reached over to touch his hand on the rail, almost expecting her fingers to go right through his. They didn't. His hand was as solid as hers, but cooler to the touch. "Thank you. You've done so much for me, and you didn't have to. I'm sorry I yelled at you earlier. And I'm sorry I can't be everything you want me to be. It's not that I don't want to."

"Madeleine," he said, facing her and turning her so that he could hold her shoulders. "You are. You're headstrong, loving, self-sacrificing and innately good. You won't lose that even if you never wear a golden halo. It's all right."

She nodded, tears stinging her eyes. "Thank you. Can I... Can I give you a hug?"

"You'd better."

She didn't know exactly where to put her arms, because his wings were in the way. But she managed. Maybe some of his light would rub off on her, because she needed it.

Inside the bedroom, Ash was waiting, giving them some privacy. His expression was dark, and he and Riam exchanged curt nods as Riam left the room, leaving them alone.

God, she did love him. He seemed to cast a shadow over the room's pale, pastel décor as they regarded each other across the slight distance between them. Then he opened his arms, and she rushed into them, clinging desperately to him and giving release to the tears she'd managed to hold in with Riam.

"Make love to me," she whispered. "I need to be with you one last time...like this."

No sooner had the words left her mouth than his lips met hers. Then clothes were coming off, a slow revealing she knew both of them savored. She gasped and bit down on a curse when she saw the marks and bruises on his flesh, fresh tears brimming in her eyes though she'd thought she couldn't shed any more.

"They hurt you," she said, trailing her fingertips over an angry red welt with the barest of brushes.

"Already healing." He took another brief taste of her lips. "I'm resilient. All I could think of was getting back to you."

"Oh, Ash, I love you." She didn't know how to say what she meant without sounding incredibly mushy, that she wanted to give him all the love he'd never had. So she tried to show him with her kiss, the gentleness of her touch on his wounds. There were so many she could hardly touch him at all without brushing against one. But he never winced, never drew away

189

from her. If anything, he only grew more impassioned.

He kissed her and caressed her until she ached, until her legs gave and he lowered her to the bed. Her breasts, her thighs, her belly...he subjected them all to a slow exploration, deliberately avoiding the needy place between her legs until she wanted to scream with frustration. When finally he did venture there, he found her slick and ready. He waited until that desperate, frenzied moment when the tip of his cock was poised at her entrance before he returned her words.

"I love you, Madeleine." And he sank into her, smothering her cry with his kiss. With slow, smooth strokes, he nudged her to the edge of bliss and sent her tumbling into its welcome depths again and again. It was thrilling with no barriers between them. When he came, she felt it, loved the sensation of him spilling into her as he shuddered and groaned in her ear, and she found a completeness with him she hadn't quite realized had been missing before. She knew just who he was now, what he was.

In the sweet moments afterward, as they lay catching their breath, he placed his hand against her cheek. "I had it all wrong."

"Hmm?"

"I was wrong. I always looked at it as if you belonged to me. It was the other way around all this time. I belong to you. If I had a soul, you stole it centuries ago."

She smiled dreamily at him, letting herself get lost in his dark eyes. Whatever they would face tonight, they'd face it together. It was going to work. It had to. "No matter what I said the other day in my apartment, I'm yours, Ash. This is one soul you didn't have to steal."

"Well, here we are," Maddie said with a little laugh a couple hours later. She and Ash sat on the bed facing each other. Riam stood silently beside her. Maddie would've happily stayed in bed with Ash for the rest of the night—or the rest of her life—but it was time to see if her crazy plan would work.

Ash nodded. "After everything we've been through, I never thought it would come to this."

She reached up and laid her palm against the side of his face. He automatically turned his head to kiss it. "It's going to be all right," she said. "Don't you think so?"

Ash's eyes had never reflected light, something she'd noticed with some curiosity a few times. Now, she swore she could see something shining in them. "If I didn't think there was a chance, I wouldn't do it."

"Okay." Somehow that made her feel better, that he had even a modicum of hope. "I'm ready."

More than anything, she was afraid of feeling the way she had when that other demon had attacked her—the horrific, scalding pain was still a fresh memory. Ash must've been reading her thoughts as he took her hand. He looked deep into her eyes and she tried to draw upon the strength she saw there.

"It'll only hurt until you're detached. Once you're completely pulled free, you won't feel anything."

Panic set off inside her as she remembered floating in a black void of numbness. "Will I be able to see or hear—"

"Yes, although not the way you're accustomed to seeing and hearing now. You'll sense your surroundings, though. You'll know I'm with you."

She nodded, taking a deep, steadying breath. "Okay."

"Take my hand," Riam said. She obeyed, still holding on to Ash with her other. It was an odd sensation, touching both of them: one hot, the other cool. A strange energy zinged through her.

"Please make it fast," she said, hating how small and pleading and cowardly she sounded all of a sudden.

Ash's gaze never left hers. His black eyes seemed to fill her universe. Power was rising there. She could see it. At the last instant, she instinctively wanted to throw herself away from him, but he didn't give her a chance. His free hand shot to her chest and everything within her tore loose. She had a moment to emit one cry at the agony of it, then his fingers dug into her flesh, twisted and pulled...and it was over.

For a moment, everything was dim, blurry and distant. She heard voices—Ash saying "I've got you, it's all right." Riam telling him to hurry—he didn't have much time. There was no opportunity to get accustomed to the strangeness of it. Suddenly she was falling. Wind rushing all around her. The longer it went on, the more aware she became of his arms locked around her, holding her to the steady anchor of his body in the maelstrom. So fast, they were going so fast, surely when they hit the bottom...

It seemed as if it would never come, as if she'd go on falling forever. In truth it probably lasted only a few minutes. Then, all at once, it stopped. Everything...stopped.

"Madeleine, look," Ash said, his voice near her ear—did she have ears? Did she have eyes? How could she look? It was all dark...

He pulled away from her and she realized it was dark because her face had been crammed against his chest. Here, she felt solid, she felt real again. That stood to reason, she supposed, if a soul was capable of feeling the torment promised in this place.

Madeleine obeyed Ash's command, looked around—and

fought not to shove her face back into his chest.

Horror all around her. They stood on a craggy outcropping in the vicinity of a huge...castle, she supposed, though she'd never seen anything like it in her life, even in art. Impossible architecture, a hodgepodge of *could not be*, with its stairs and doors leading to nowhere.

Above it all, black clouds seethed. Lightning flickered orange and red. Below them...fire. Only fire. The landscape beyond the keep, as far as she could see, was made of charred rock and what appeared to be lava, and...

The faces in the mirrors. The dead-eyed souls, as she'd described them to Ash before. The things she'd been afraid were going to get her someday. They were everywhere, crawling, trying to escape the flames, being pulled back in by some unseen force.

It was every nightmare she'd ever had, come to searing life.

"This is my home," Ash said, his voice sharp. She looked at him and saw his eyes did reflect the light here, such as it was. It glowed and flickered, a perfect reflection of the inferno around them.

She tried to take a deep breath and found that she couldn't. What was there to breathe here, anyway? The fumes had to be toxic, but it didn't matter, because try as she might, she couldn't suck it in. Desperately, she clawed at her uncooperative throat, a resurgence of panic overtaking her.

Ash noticed her distress and grasped her hands, pulling them away and holding them. "Madeleine, you don't have to breathe. You have no functioning lungs, you have no beating heart. You have only the memory of these things. Just relax, let go. You aren't going to suffocate. You can't."

You're dead, she finished for him. Oh, dear God, she'd really done it, she'd let him kill her. How could she trust him

193

that much? What if it had all been some elaborate ploy?

She couldn't let herself think like that. This was Ash, this was who he was, where he was from, and she loved him. He'd had the courage to show her everything. She loved him even more for that.

"Who are they?" she asked over the bubbling, boiling noises around them. She was watching the ghastly spirits in the flames.

"The damned," he answered simply. "The worst of the worst."

"They're the ones I always saw haunting me."

"I figured."

If she were honest with herself, she'd know she wanted to stand there clinging to him from now on out of fear if she moved, something out there would get her. But she straightened and lifted her chin, looking up at him. "Ash, it's terrible here. You're right about that. But it's not enough to scare me away."

A muscle clenched in his jaw. "You haven't seen everything yet."

She would've swallowed, if her throat had worked. He stepped backward away from her, desolation in his orange-black eyes. Maddie held on to his hand until he'd moved too far away, and she let hers drop.

"What haven't I seen?" she asked, not liking how small and tinny her voice sounded.

"You haven't seen me."

The very air—or whatever there was here—seemed to shudder around him, dark smoky tendrils forming and encircling him like a slow whirlwind. Finally it engulfed him fully, until he was a pillar of what she could only describe as black light. It grew, stretching upward another foot or so over his regular height. It spread outward, forming vast winglike shapes on either side of his shoulders. When it slowly began to dissipate...

Her knees wanted to give. She wanted to fall to them and weep. Tell him that was it, she'd had enough, take her home now. The thing he'd become before her very eyes was something she didn't think human eyes were meant to behold. She received only a mere impression: blackened scales, leathery webbed wings, terrible black claws for hands...and she had to look down.

"Madeleine," he said, and though his voice was deeper, growling, distorted...she still heard *Ash* in there. He stepped closer. "Look at me. Look at what you were prepared to spend eternity with."

She found something she could still do was cry. Maybe demons left them that ability for a reason. Maybe they liked to see the tears of their victims. The droplets fell from her eyes, sizzling and smoking where they landed on the scorched earth under her feet. Capturing her lower lip between her teeth, she lifted her gaze back to him. She owed him that much.

Just as she'd heard the Ash she knew in his voice, she could see him in his face too. The brow she'd caressed, only heavily ridged...and sprouting curled horns like a ram's. The eyes she'd looked into, only bigger and darker. The mouth she'd kissed. And now she noticed his wings were torn...part of his torture? Dark wounds striped his broad, heavily muscled chest.

Anger simmered bright and hot in her chest. They'd taken this strong, indomitable creature and humiliated him, tormented him over her, and he'd taken it. He'd *let* them. Because she couldn't fathom how they had overpowered him, no matter how many of them there were.

Regardless of how he appeared to her now, he was still the being who'd held her when she was afraid. Who'd laughed with her and made her feel better. Who'd chased away the nightmares—even though he'd been the reason for them in the first place.

"Just let me go to my fate," he said. "Let me take you back. Forget about me and live your life, as I told you before."

She closed the distance between them. It wasn't easy, looking up into the face of a seven-and-a-half-foot demon, but she managed. She put her hands on his chest, leaned forward and kissed one of his terrible wounds. He growled out her name despairingly, and rested one of his huge hands on the top of her head with such gentleness it only made her tears come harder. She tilted her head back and looked up at him.

"I'm not running yet," she said. "So what else have you got?"

With a strangled sound, he dropped to his knees before her. As big as he was, that only put his head in the vicinity of her throat. "*Please*," he said, gripping her arms. She never would have thought to see such an expression of heartbreak on the face of...of a monster, but there it was. It wrenched everything within her. "You can't stay here."

"Ash," she whispered, gently touching both sides of his face. His skin was hard and rough but sensitive; the muscles jumped under her fingers. "I have to save you. It's not about me. Don't you understand? If it's even possible that your bringing me here will spare your life, I have to try. I'm *going* to. There's nothing you can say, nothing you can show me, that's going to change that."

She pulled his head toward her, wrapped her arms around it and leaned her cheek against him. Slowly, his hold on her relaxed, and his arms went around her waist so tightly she could hardly...well, she couldn't breathe anyway, could she? And it was a good thing, because his grip wouldn't have allowed it. All the fight seemed to go out of him and resignation settled in its place. She could see it in the droop of his mighty shoulders.

"I love you," she whispered, her tears dripping onto his head. She swore the very ground beneath her trembled when she said it.

Chapter Seventeen

That Madeleine should see where he came from, that she should see *him*, was insufferable. He should just seize her and take her back to her waiting body, which Riam was helping keep animated for her return. He'd insisted upon that much. But it didn't buy much time—maybe an hour or so. And time was so unpredictable here. If he didn't get her back soon, their entire debate would be moot. It would be too late.

He knew all of this. Still, he hadn't done it.

What if it worked? What if she could stay here and be his? If she'd seen it and she was willing to face it, to give up everything for it—what arguments were there left to make?

He stood and led her wordlessly toward the keep. The only way this would work was for Metos to see her, approve her admittance and declare Ash spared. Funny how all of Hell was around him and his heart felt like a chunk of ice rattling in his chest. He'd be lucky if Riam didn't put his little amulet to use and seek him out to give him a good trashing. The thought made his lips quirk. He'd probably let him, at this point.

Conditions didn't improve on the inside of the keep; if anything, they were more deplorable. All he could do was steer Madeleine straight ahead, keep her moving, try to prevent her from examining any passing chambers too closely. If she insisted on being here, he would do his damnedest to protect her from as many of the horrors as he could.

If they let him live.

Screams sounded in the distance, and she started with each one. Even he didn't like the sound, imagining the time he'd spent hanging helpless and blind in the dungeon. They *would* have to kill him before they stuck him back in there. He hoped Metos was ready for a fight if their plan didn't work.

They reached the massive doors that led to Metos's chamber, and Ash turned Madeleine to face him. "This is it. Are you ready?"

"No, but I don't have a choice."

He managed a smile for her. Here she was a faded image of herself, but still so beautiful he ached. At the moment, he could not even fathom that there had ever been a time when he wanted this for her.

He had so much to make up for. And he wanted to get started.

"Let me do the talking. Whatever I say, go along. Show as little weakness or fear as you can," he told her. "They feed on it, thrive on it. They'll be like bloodhounds picking up a scent, understand?" She nodded. "Then let's go."

He took her arm and shoved his way through the doors. Metos, sitting on his ridiculous throne, was holding court with a number of the other Masters. Saklon, that bastard, was one of them. Madeleine's step faltered as she spied him and, as much as Ash wanted to reassure her in some way, he kept her moving. A tiny sob escaped her, but she complied.

His superior's chamber was dark and vast, like almost every other room in this place. The corners dissolved into the flickering shadows cast by the torches and fire pots. Their steps echoed through the hall, through the absolute silence that had descended upon their entrance. All eyes turned toward them, some humanoid, others beastly. Madeleine ground in her heels and he pushed her ahead of him, wanting more than anything to jerk her into the safety of his arms. But they had to hold it together these first few minutes or they might not make it another step.

Metos's brow rose with interest. He lifted a finger pensively to his lips. "Well, well."

"You wanted me to take her," Ash said. He hauled Madeleine in front of the throne as the others silently made way for them. "Here she is."

"I'm glad to see you've come back to your senses." Metos rose from his chair and descended the dais. Madeleine pushed back against Ash's hand, recoiling as the other demon slowly approached, but Ash held her steady in front of him. His master's yellow eyes burned as they swept hungrily over her figure, and every protective instinct Ash possessed screamed in answering rage.

When the bastard lifted a long finger to touch her cheek, Ash jerked her back, encircling her with his arm and holding her tight against him. "No."

Metos's eyes narrowed further.

"It's the only request I make." He couldn't resist casting a narrow glare in Saklon's direction. "Let her be mine, and only mine. To do with as I wish."

"Where's the fun in that?" Saklon asked, getting a chuckle from the others.

Metos's arm fell by his side. "I should have known you would be selfish with this one. It'll be disappointing if she can't receive all of our...attentions to welcome her."

Yeah, too bad about that, fucker. Madeleine was shuddering against him. "I can always return her if my conditions aren't met. Angels are waiting to place her under divine protection

200

when I do. That would mean death to any demon who touches her."

The entire room seemed to freeze. Metos had been walking a slow circle around them...even he paused mid-step for an instant. Then he whirled around, his black cape swirling around his legs. "What do you mean, return her?"

Damn. "Exactly what I said. Truth be known, I brought her here fully intending to take her back." Madeleine turned an incredulous look on him, but he ignored it.

Metos's yellow gaze dropped to Madeleine. "Then what is she doing here now?"

This hadn't really gone in the direction Ash had planned.

"I'm here because I want to be," Madeleine said quietly. Ash closed his eyes, biting down on a curse. He tightened his grip on her in warning, though it wouldn't do any good. "I'm here because I love him."

Every demon in the room recoiled. Even the earth itself seemed to react, trembling under their feet, just as the first time she'd said it outside the keep.

"No." Metos was shaking head, quivering in outrage. His gaze whipped back to Ash, quick like the flickers of flame around them. "What have you done? You *fool*."

Thou shalt purge the abomination, banish the afflicted, for it is an offense Hell cannot deign to hold.

Suddenly, the words Ash had read in Metos's study, which had puzzled him at the time, leaped into his head and rocked him to the core. They made perfect sense now. Here, an abomination Hell couldn't hold was the opposite of everything it stood for. It was...love.

And Metos had been studying the rule. It had even been wedged into Madeleine's book.

What had he done, indeed?

"You threaten our very foundations bringing her here like this! Is that what you want, Ashemnon?"

"I only want her. However I can have her."

"I knew of *your* idiotic infatuation, but Hell cannot suffer a soul capable of loving the unlovable."

"I'm here by my own agreement. Even my own wishes," Madeleine said.

Metos ignored her. "I should kill you for this," he snarled at Ash.

"You're always saying you should kill me for one reason or another," Ash said. "Isn't it about time you quit talking and got on with it?"

Metos glowered a moment longer and then lifted his arm. Ash considered the fact he should have kept his mouth shut. In his master's hand, a flaming orange sword formed, glowing bright and deadly and making the room seem even darker. Madeleine pushed against his side, but he nudged her away, assuming his own battle stance and facing his once-friend and superior.

"So we've let it come to this?" Ash asked, pulling his own fiery weapon of choice from the superheated atmosphere: an executioner's axe. It felt good in his hand, heavy and lethal. He hefted it in both hands, preparing to block Metos's first blows with the sturdy handle.

"*You've* let it come to this," Metos said as they slowly circled each other. "I wish I had time to do the job properly, to make you suffer...but I grow weary of your games. I'll kill you quick, and she'll become excellent entertainment for my hall."

"You'll die for those words alone."

"And once I'm dead? Look around you. You haven't the

strength to fight every demon in this room, minion. If I fall, there will be many to replace me."

"As if I expect them to stand idly even before I kill you. No, you wouldn't have honor enough to fight fairly."

"Have you forgotten where you are?" With that, Metos rushed. Their weapons clashed, sparks flying as they traded one blow after another. They were well matched, a little too well. Madeleine shrieked and gasped from the side of their battle, more distracting than anything else. He could only hope none of the others grabbed her, or he would absolutely lose his mind. And most likely this fight.

Metos lunged straight for Ash's chest with the tip of his blade. Ash parried, swinging low as he did so and sweeping Metos's legs from under him. The other demon fell hard, immediately rolling away as Ash brought down his axe. The blow glanced harmlessly off the floor. Dammit, he wasn't going to defeat anyone if he couldn't do better than that. He leaped to avoid Metos's answering sword thrust, and the other demon took the opportunity to kick him in the knee as he came down. He went to the floor, ignoring the agony and attacking his master with his bare hands.

They rolled, snarling and slashing, tearing bloody strips from each other's flesh. It was no use; hand to hand, Metos was far stronger. But when Ash heard Madeleine yelp and saw that one of the others had his filthy claws on her, he found the strength to get his legs under Metos's body and shove upward with all his might. Metos flew off him, falling to the side and rolling. Ash leaped up and rushed at the demon pawing at Madeleine. He threw her down with a growl and braced himself for the attack. Ash slammed into him, taking them both to the ground.

Madeleine screamed his name. The ground rumbled

beneath them, the tremor far stronger than the two before it had been.

Metos was right; Ash couldn't take them all. Despair settled on him as heavily as the weakness beginning to lap at his limbs. Fury was a mighty motivator, but it would take one only so far. Before long, he would begin to burn out, and now Metos was getting a breather. It would go that way until Ash was exhausted.

It didn't matter. He would fight until he couldn't move anymore, but maybe it was time to switch strategies and employ the best weapon he'd always had: his mouth.

Struggling his way out from under the other demon, he scrambled to his feet and gave him a hard kick for good measure. Metos was advancing on him again. Ash sidestepped him and walked backward, forcing his master to stalk him.

"Did you feel that?" Ash asked. "Every time she opens her mouth, she brings potential catastrophe. Because of her love for me."

"I'm going to test a theory. It's only when you're together that you're a danger to us here. Without you to direct her pathetic love *to*, she won't be a problem."

"But what if she is? What if you're wrong? What if by killing me, you'll unleash such anguish in her that she—one seemingly inconsequential soul—will bring all of Hell to its knees?" He grinned. He was sure it was a bloody one. "She certainly brought me to mine, and I'm not ashamed to admit it."

"You're useless."

"Am I? Shall I ask her right now to tell me she loves me again? And again and again? What will be left of your precious hall then? I'll tell you. A pile of rubble."

"You aren't going to make me honestly think she can—"

"But you don't know. Do you? I saw the little rule in your study. I didn't know what it meant at the time. You're to 'purge' us. Why is that, Metos? If we weren't such a threat, why couldn't we stay? It's as you said...we're a catastrophe waiting to happen. You know it."

Metos stopped advancing on him. His flaming sword dissipated as if it had never been. For a long moment, he stared at Ash, who didn't dare to relax for fear of some unforeseen attack. Finally, Metos opened his mouth, pausing for a moment before speaking as if choosing his words carefully. "You...are not even worthy of death."

"There's a new one."

"Get out of my sight. Ashemnon, you are banished forthwith from the kingdom of the Dark Lord. Go live with your concubine and see how well her world accepts you." He gave a dismissive wave of his hand and turned his back, trudging back to his throne. "See how long before you're begging me to come back home."

Ash was afraid to move, afraid to hope. From her place on the floor where she'd landed, Madeleine turned round eyes on him, aghast. He must not have been hearing things, then— she'd heard it too. "We can go?" she mouthed to him.

"Go!" Metos all but roared. "Remove her before she destroys us all!"

He didn't have to say it again. Ash grabbed Madeleine's hand, yanked her up and got her the hell out of there, hiding a grin the whole way. His little angel, whether she wanted to be or not.

It felt good, so good, to be normal again. She'd said she would stay there with Ash, and she'd meant it...but damn, she was glad she didn't have to. Waking up here had been like resurfacing from one of her nightmares, so profoundly glad to be awake and alive it was almost painful.

Riam looked as eager as a kid on Christmas as she opened her eyes, and Ash hung his head in relief. His very *human*-looking head, thank goodness. Both of them held her hands, and Ash's other hand was on her chest. Bringing her back to life, again.

"Well?" Riam asked.

"Apparently, I nearly destroyed Hell," Madeleine told him.

Ash laughed and Riam rolled his eyes heavenward. "Dear God, if only we could be so lucky."

"I was banished," Ash said. "All around, it was a most productive trip."

"Banished? Interesting. Hell doesn't want you and Heaven won't have you. What will you do?"

"Stay here, I suppose." He looked down into Madeleine's eyes. She saw the weariness in his and thought maybe she'd like to add to it, but in a far more pleasurable way than they had just experienced. Later. For now, she smiled and squeezed his hand. "Be loved, surely," he finished.

"That much is for certain," she said.

"You know," Riam said, looking thoughtful, "Celeste can help you get everything you need to exist among the mortals. If you're truly no longer one of Hell's minions, I don't see what harm it will do for us to assist you."

"Really?" Madeleine asked. She struggled to sit up, but the two of them had to help her. Even so, overall she felt much better than she had the last time Ash had brought her back. "We need to figure this out. You're banished, but you're not human. You're still immortal...right?"

"It would appear so," Ash said. "I still had the ability to bring you back, so I haven't been stripped of my power or anything."

"Am I really going to have to get old and gray while you still look like...*this*? Not that I'm complaining," she amended quickly when Ash turned an incredulous look toward her. "It'll just...cause problems, you know?"

"Not when I can appear any age I want." He grinned at her. "I just prefer this one. But if you need me to look like a wrinkled old man someday, I can do that. For you."

"Thanks...I guess." She giggled, until another thought cast a shadow across her jubilation. "But what about...after I'm gone?"

"Well, let's not dwell on that now," Riam said with determined optimism. "Go and have a long and happy life together—it's more than most people get. We'll figure that out when the time comes. I'll still be around, of course." He gave Madeleine a wink, the gesture so out of place on him that she lifted a brow at him.

A long and happy life. She liked the sound of that. It sounded much better than a dark and miserable eternity.

Epilogue

"Are you sure you want to do this?" Ash asked.

"No. But it's something I need to do. Thanks for coming with me." She knocked for the third time on the door they were standing in front of. Maybe he wasn't home. Maybe he didn't answer the door for strangers. Maybe they'd come all this way for nothing.

"Of course. He's not going to be happy to see me, though." Ash turned and faced the quiet street behind them, muttering to himself. "Probably have a heart attack."

Maybe he didn't open the door for demons who'd enticed him to trade his daughter's soul almost thirty years ago. Yeah, that could be it.

"Well, for that matter, he might not be happy to see *me*."

"I can go sit in the car, if you think it would help."

"No." She reached over and took his gloved hand with her own. It was brutally cold out and snow dusted the carefully tended yards and their tacky Christmas embellishments. Her dad's yard boasted Santa waving from his sleigh, while the simple but cute frame house was liberally draped with twinkling colored lights. "I want you here."

Ash looked over at her and smiled. She took a moment, as she often did, to appreciate how beautiful he was, his dark hair glistening with tiny ice crystals. The past couple of years with him had been the happiest of her entire life, and that happiness didn't appear to be letting up anytime soon.

This was a crazy scheme if ever there was one. But if what Ash said was true, and her father had turned his life around after making the deal with him all those years ago, then he must carry tremendous guilt. Ash had described what kind of person he'd been. He also knew what kind of person he'd become—one who'd kicked the drugs, helped out in his community, and counseled runaways and other troubled youth. Even Riam had been a source of information. Heaven had been keeping its watchful eye on Maxwell Gatlin. But something else Riam had told her was that her dad was sick now and wasn't long for this world.

Yes, it was a terrible thing he'd done. But she wanted to give him what peace she could before he left. She wanted him to know she was okay, that he'd inadvertently done her a wonderful favor.

Of course, it had to be jarring, knowing a family member was happily in love with a creature of darkness. If you cared at all, anyway.

It was another thing she had to consider, that he wouldn't give a rat's ass if she was dead or alive or burning in Hell by now. She simply couldn't bring herself to believe he'd feel that way, however.

Fueled by urgency at the thought, she pounded on the door again, harder than she had before. She had to know. She didn't know why it was so important, but it was. It kept her up at night, talking to Ash deep into the wee hours. He was the one who'd told her maybe it would be good for her to face him. She'd always entertained the thought, but it hadn't seemed plausible, or something she would *really* consider doing, until he suggested it.

Suddenly, the door swung open while she was mid-knock. Maddie froze, lowering her arm. Ash turned around. An older woman with tidy graying hair stood framed by the doorway, head cocked to the side as she appraised them with shrewd eyes. "Yes?"

"Um, hello," Maddie said. "Does Maxwell Gatlin live here?"

"He does. May I say who's calling?"

"My name is Madeleine Dean. He may not know me, but..." She took a deep breath. "I'm his daughter."

The woman looked her up and down, pulling her green cardigan closer against the cold rushing into the house. Madeleine wanted to huddle closer to the heat pouring out. "You're Madeleine?"

"You...know my name?"

"Honey, he's talked about having a daughter named Madeleine for as long as I've known him—that would be twenty-five years, now. But he never knew your last name, or how to reach you at all. I always wondered if you really existed."

"And you are...?"

"I'm his wife. Please call me Anne." She offered her hand, still looking shell-shocked, and Madeleine shook it, feeling the same. This was surreal. Anne glanced back into the house. "I'm afraid he's not doing so well at the moment."

"I had heard he was ill. I'm terribly sorry."

Anne nodded, removing the silver-framed glasses she'd been wearing and wiping her eyes before replacing them. "I'm sorry, this is just so..."

Madeleine reached over and touched her arm. "I know."

Composing herself, Anne went on. "Yes, he has cancer. The doctors, they're still trying, but things aren't looking too well this time. The treatments take a lot out of him and he's resting. But I know he would be so upset if I didn't tell him you were here."

"I don't want to disturb him—"

"Nonsense. Come in out of the cold before you freeze." She held her arm out toward Ash and ushered them both inside. "And who is this handsome fellow? Your husband, surely?"

Just my demon lover.

"Oh, something like that," he said. Madeleine bit her lip on a smile. "Call me Ash."

She looked around the living room as they traded pleasantries. Though outside it was nearly dusk, the scent of coffee drifted in from the kitchen. It was nice and homey here, the end tables and walls crowded with pictures of loved ones. At least he seemed to have lived a life full of happiness.

She hoped she'd get the opportunity to meet some of the faces in those photos, the family she'd never known. Maybe they would be closer to her than the one she'd had. Maybe.

"He had some strange stories to tell," Anne was saying a little nervously when Madeleine turned her attention back to her. "He never could really explain how he knew about you, or knew your name at all. At least, he would never tell me. I suspected he had more to say, he just wouldn't say it. But come to think of it...for some reason he believed something might have happened to you. Lord, honey, you can probably help answer a thousand of my questions he's turned aside over the years."

"I'll be happy to," she said, casting a glance at Ash.

"Please, have a seat. I'll let him know you're here." Anne indicated the afghan-covered couch and slipped quietly from the room.

211

"I think you probably *should* wait out here," Madeleine whispered to Ash. "I mean, if I get to go back and see him."

He nodded, pulling her into his arms. "That would be best."

She breathed in his scent, wrapping herself in the comforting warmth of his embrace. "If it wasn't for you, he wouldn't know my name, would he? He wouldn't know about me at all."

"I guess not," he murmured. "I told him about you."

"My mom knew who he was, but as far as I know, she never even attempted to contact him. No one did."

Ash kissed her forehead just as Anne came back into the room.

"Madeleine? You'll have to come on back here, but he's so excited to meet you."

Madeleine left Ash's embrace and moved away, holding one of his hands as long as she could before she had to let it go. He smiled at her, and again, she thought she could see something shining in his eyes. "Thank you," she mouthed to him, and followed Anne down the hall.

About the Author

If Cherrie Lynn's parents are to be believed, she's been writing since before she can remember. Through her formative years, her stories evolved from epic graphic novels about dragons and unicorns to middle school angst-inspired teen soap operas. Once she discovered her mom's romance novels, she finally found her place.

She adores electronic gadgets, heavy metal, gaming, and horror movies. You can often find her traveling far and wide to catch her favorite rock acts live, but she's much too fragile to go near a mosh pit.

Cherrie lives in Texas with her husband and two kids. She loves hearing from readers, so drop her a line at cherrie@cherrielynn.com or visit her at www.cherrielynn.com.

She has Heaven to lose. He has Hell to pay.

Sweet Disgrace
© *2010 Cherrie Lynn*

Centuries of heartbreak. Grinding failures punctuated by too-few victories. What angel in her right mind would want this job? Celeste, who's driven to save Devil-contracted souls before Hell can claim them, is weary, but not beaten. Yet.

Her latest case makes her wonder if it's all worth the anguish. A demon enticed a too-young musician into selling his soul for fortune and fame. To make matters worse, that demon is Damael, an insufferable, frightening minion with airtight contracts—and a body that makes her long for sin.

Damael's always had a soft spot for Celeste, but if his bored superiors want drama, he'll give them drama. Though it pains him to trick the angel he wants with all his black heart, eons of restrained lust win out. He makes the deal: her body in exchange for the human's soul.

She wasn't supposed to accept.

Damael can't be trusted, but with the deadline bearing down, Celeste lays everything on the line in a last-ditch effort to save just one precious soul. Even if it means losing hers—along with her heart.

Warning: This title contains graphic language, explicit sex, an angelic heroine with attitude...and a demonic hero who's smoking hot. Literally.

Available now in ebook from Samhain Publishing.

www.samhainpublishing.com

Green for the planet.
Great for your wallet.

It's all about the story...

Romance

HORROR

www.samhainpublishing.com